CALIBRE

Also by Ken Bruen

Funeral

Shades of Grace

Martyrs

Rilke on Black

The Hackman Blues

Her Last Call to Louis MacNeice

A White Arrest

Taming the Alien

The McDead

London Boulevard

The Guards

The Killing of the Tinkers

Blitz

The Magdalen Martyrs

Vixen

The Dramatist

KEN BRUEN
CALIBRE

 St. Martin's Minotaur ✹ New York

www.minotaurbooks.com

Library of Congress Cataloging-in-Publication Data

Bruen, Ken.
    Calibre / Ken Bruen.
        p. cm.
     ISBN-13: 978-0-312-34144-2
     ISBN-10: 0-312-34144-X
     1. Brant, Detective Sergeant (Ficticious character)—Fiction. 2. Police—England—London—Fiction. 3. London (England)—Fiction. 4. Serial murderers—Fiction. 5. Psychopaths—Fiction. I. Title.

   PR6052.R785C35 2006
   823'.914—dc22

                               2006040503

First Edition: August 2006

10   9   8   7   6   5   4   3   2   1

FOR MAGGIE GRIFFIN
AL GUTHRIE
DAVID CORBETT

"Huh-uh," he said. "You got it wrong."

—Jim Thompson, *The Killer Inside Me*

1

SHIT FROM SHINOLA. You have to hand it to the god-
damn Yanks, they have great verbals, man. I love the way
they cuss.

I killed my first last Tuesday, I can't believe it was so easy.
Remorse? Not a fuckin' trace. Only sorry I didn't do it
sooner.

I'm forty-four years old, and I guess I'm what you'd call a
late starter. Or as them Yanks have it, a late bloomer. Thirty
years I could have been mowing down the fucks and what
was I doing?

Working.

A working stiff.

I think it was Bob Geldof who said work was the biggest
con of all. I listen to The Rats with 'I Don't Like Mondays'
and I've got my soundtrack down. They nailed it. The silicon
chip inside my head just switched to overload.

Been a long time coming.

My old man, Anthony Crew, worked in an asbestos fac-
tory all his life. The last ten years he spent coughing up blood

and gook till his eyes bulged. His employers, did they cover the hospital bills? They did fuck-all.

The National Health Service did the best they could but he was fucked and gone; he was dead and didn't know it, wouldn't lie down. The Mick in him, those Paddies, tough sons of bitches. Every Sunday I went round his gaff, a council flat on Railton Road, and listened to him cough. James Joyce is buried in Switzerland near a zoo, and his wife, Nora Barnacle, said:

'He liked to listen to the lions roar.' Brixton is as close to a zoo as it gets. My dad, his face contorted to grotesque degrees of agony, and I wanted to kill some fucker.

Now I have:

> Willeford
> Woolich
> Thompson.

My heroes. I've read crime fiction for over twenty years, can't get enough, black as it's painted. The classic hard-boiled, though, these guys are the biz.

Noir and out.

Shit-kickers par excellence. My bookcase is an homage to pulp:

> James M. Cain
> Hammett
> Chandler.

Here's a thing. I can't read Chandler's novels any more, but his letters, phew-oh, now you're cooking. They're on my bedside table, resting on my old man's Bible. His book passed down through generations of navvies to land here in Clapham. Could be worse, could be Kilburn.

Might be yet.

Used to be if you were in a hotel and wanted a hooker, open the Gideon Bible back page, bingo. Not any more. I blame the Internet, all that cybersex and chat rooms, they've taken the zing out of dirt.

I'm not going to get caught. I'm due for another kill on Friday, a woman this time, keep the balance. The reason I won't get caught is not just cos I'm smart but I have an edge.

I watch *CSI*.

STUDY IT.

So I'm au fait . . . With all the DNA fibres, signatures, trophies, crap. Two things in my corner, I'm random and I'm careful.

Hard to top.

They won't.

I've read the true crime books, from Ann Rule through Joe McGinnis to Jack Olsen. Man I know my shit. Am I a psychopath? A sociopath? A paranoid schizophrenic? A narcissistic disorder? A blip on the human radar?

Who the fuck cares. What I am is good and angry, like Peter Finch in *Network*. You think you can label me, tame me?

Dream on, sucker.

I'm the pale rider of Clapham.

But hey, let's get it down. I'm not into weird shit. None of that cannibalism or jerking off on bodies. Jeez, I hate that stuff. Truth to tell, I can't even read about it. And child molesters? Don't get me started.

Kids? Would I kill a kid? No way, José. Not unless he was in a boy band.

This is my reality TV. Killing for prime time.

Here's another thing, hope you're taking notes cos, like, I'll be asking questions. Ever see that profiler shine they pedal? Me now, they'd typically pin as:

White (true)
Late twenties, early thirties (wrong)
Loner (mm . . . mmm)
Isolated (nope)
Impotent (hey!)
Narcissistic (well okay, I'll give 'em that)
Low-paying job (nope)
No partner (wrong again)
Quiet (I'm a party animal).

You want to know how they catch serials?

Luck, dumb friggin' luck. Bundy got stopped for a busted tail-light. I don't have a damaged vehicle, no sirree. I've got cash; and if I ever get stupid, I'll get a pick-up, a hound dog, and a shitpile of Hank Williams.

Music.

You ever hear of a killer into tunes? Apart from looney ones? I listen to music all the time.

But Time Out.

Not the mag, me. I'm beat. This writing isn't as easy as the pulpists would lead you to think. I'm learning the craft from Chandler's letters. All you ever need to know, he not only tells you how but why.

Oh and another reason the dumb fucks keep getting apprehended? Someone drops a dime. The Irish disease, like alcoholism, is ratting out. They invented Guinness but also the fink.

So don't talk. You don't talk, there's nothing to rat out. 'Loose lips sink ships.'

Gotta get some zzzz's.

And I'm not lazy, whatever else I am. I'll tell you everything.
—Jim Thompson, *The Killer Inside Me*

2

SERGEANT BRANT WAS in the canteen. Slung over the back of his chair was a Driza-Bone jacket. He was licking the chocolate off a Club Milk; the sounds he made were deliberately loud, exaggerated, and having the desired effect. Cops at nearby tables were aware of him, powerless to shout:

'For fucksakes!'

Brant was a pig, worked at it. He was heavily built with a black Irish face that wasn't so much lived in as squatted upon. He was wearing a very expensive suit that whispered:

'Serious wedge.'

He had numerous schemes running, all illegal, that kept him in a style ill-suited to a sergeant in the SE London Met. The brass knew he was dirty, he knew they knew, but proof remained elusive.

Superintendent Brown had tried for years to shaft him.

Unsuccessfully.

Brant was deeply tan. Another feature not common to cops. He'd wrangled his way onto a Police Exchange Scheme in Australia and spent two weeks in Sydney. To annoy his immediate superior, Chief Inspector Roberts, he now littered his speech with Strine, Oz slang. Roberts, seriously irritated by Brant's chocolate slurping, moved his own tea aside, said:

'We better get a move on.'

Brant now wished he'd dunked the last of his Club Milk in his tea, few things matched the melting chocolate rush. He reached in his jacket, took out a pack of Peter Jackson, a twenty-five box, as is the norm in Oz. Plus a battered Zippo. All over the canteen were decals, roaring:

SMOKING VERBOTEN.

Well, not in Kraut but with that tone. Roberts sighed as Brant cranked the lighter, an old inscription on the side, barely legible:

1968.

Brant smiled, not his usual wolverine but something near regret, shrugged it off, said:

'I tell you, sir, the sheilas in Oz were seriously stacked.'

The alliteration was no accident, he'd worked on it, tuned to gain max vexation.

All in the timing. Whatever else, Brant knew the value of timing. Roberts sighed, went:

'When are you going to get over Australia?'

Brant feigned hurt then:

'With all due respect, sir, you don't get over Oz. Ask Bill Bryson.'

Roberts could give a toss who Bryson was, still it was a change if not an improvement that for once Brant wasn't pushing Ed McBain. The old Penguin editions, the Eighty-seventh Precinct mysteries, Brant had owned them all, every blessed one. Till The Umpire destroyed them. An old case, never closed. Lately, Brant was obsessed with writing, fancied himself an English Joseph Wambaugh, would go:

'Money in crime . . .'

Pause.

Big delivery:

'Writing.'

Then the previous McBain, *Fat Ollie's Book,* had acceler-ated Brant's vision of the cop/author. He'd even bought *The Writers' and Artists' Year Book,* was trawling through agents and likely publishers.

Roberts asked:

'Falls back yet?'

A black WPC. The wet dream of the nick, her star had spectacularly dipped. Suspected of offing a cop killer, a spell in rehab, a near lethal coke habit, and a lesbian fling with a bomber. She was barely clinging to her job. If she'd been white, she'd been gone. Brant dropped his cig in the cup, heard the sizzle, said:

'They got her on that schools gig.'

The very bottom of the Met barrel. No, worse, out-

side the barrel, trying to reach the bottom. Certain assign-
ments:

Traffic

Railton Road nights

Press liason

Were regarded as shite, but going into classrooms, telling
apprentice muggers about the role of the police (as if they
didn't know the deal . . . cops beat on you, run your ass
ragged). This gig was regarded as the last stop before dismissal. In fact it was dismissal, bar the shouting. Consigned to
that dark side of the moon too was PC McDonald, once the
Super's golden boy and potential hatchet-man. He'd seriously fucked up and got shot into the bargain.

McDonald and Falls had a history, none of it good. They
didn't totally hate each other, but it was in the zone. Falls had
hit on a shit pile of money and sent some of it to McDonald,
anonymously, but he didn't seem to have improved in any no-
ticeable fashion. The other cops had a lottery going as to
which would crack first. The pool was a healthy £500 and
growing. If they both jacked, there was a double-indemnity
clause.

Brant asked:

'You put some money on?'

'On Falls folding?'

A little alliteration himself, it was contagious. Roberts brushed at his suit, an old number from his married days and not wearing well, said:

'I'm the Gov, how'd it be if I was betting on my squad jacking.'

Brant smiled, went:

'It'd be smart.'

They were currently tracking a stolen-car ring and pressure was on as the superintendent's Lexus had been taken. A number of false leads had increased the man's ire. One of Brant's snitches now claimed to have real information. Brant's 'informers' . . . finks, had a lethal record of getting wasted. The current one was still hanging in. Named Alcazar, known as Caz, he had a history of hanging-paper, dealing in dodgy travellers cheques. Various times he was from:

Puerto Rico
Honduras
South America.

What made him stand out from the herd was, he'd never done time.

He was short, with black hair, a dancer's body, and hooded eyes.

He was from Croydon.

And man, he could dance:

Calibre

flamenco
salsa
jive
la Macarena.

His choice of weapon was a stiletto, pearl-handled of course.
He put oceans of Brylcreem in his hair and smoked Ducados
like a good 'un.

What you might call a fully rounded individual. He wore
a huge, gold medallion of 'Our Lady of Guadalupe.'

Roberts asked:

'Who's this source we're meeting?'

Brant gave him the full wattage of his smile, said:

'You'll like him; he's a dancer.'

And she'd got it. Nothing.

—Jim Thompson, *The Killer Inside Me*

3

PORTER NASH HAD a new boyfriend.

Sorta.

Being a ranking officer and gay was not exactly usual. Plus, to add to his CV he'd recently been diagnosed with diabetes and had moved to type one. This is not an award, on the fucking contrary, it's heavy weather, you have to inject twice a day. Porter had never tried to hide his gayness. In fact he frequently paraded it through outward gestures, gestures the Carter Street cops believed proved you were gay, like menthol cigs, Barbara Streisand music, a gold bracelet, and, damning proof, a caustic tongue.

But Porter got results and impressive ones. Even Brant, a raging homophobe, gave him grudging respect. Porter had previously been gold in the prize posting of Kensington. Nirvana, the upper echelon of the Met. A question over the beating of a pædophile led to his transfer.

Initially, he'd made a close bond with Falls, a true merger of minorities, but her spectacular spiral downwards had split them. He missed her.

She detested him.

Had spat:

'You're not gay, you're ambitious.'

Even a faggot couldn't comprehend this logic. He'd asked:

'What the hell does that mean?'

She'd glared at him, sparks emphasizing the whiteness of her large eyes, radiant against the black of her skin, said:

'It means you're a prick, no pun intended.'

Gay that.

He couldn't.

The new boyfriend was named Trevor Blake. Porter had met him in a pub near the Oval. Trevor was the barman, in his late twenties, and was riding the stick.

In normal English, pulling pints.

Porter had had a rough day. The Super had carpeted him, said:

'Listen to this.'

He was holding a letter, his hands trembling with agitation. Read:

To Supt. Brown
Greetings, sir. See, I have manners. I learnt from Elvis and the novels of Daniel Buckman that manners are the finest manipulation.

Brown paused, adjusted his pince-nez, looked out over them, asked:

'Is that true?'

'Sorry, sir, is what true?'

Brown was not amused, snapped:

'About bloody manners. Don't your lot do etiquette at queer school?'

Porter felt the lash, the almost lazy bigotry, the redneck conclusion of civility with homosexuality, tried to rein in, said:

'If you mean, sir, do "Us lot" care about the feelings of others, well yes, we do have manners. As to manipulation, I couldn't rightly say.'

Pushing it.

He thought the Super was trailer trash, tried not to display so too openly. The sarcasm was wasted. It went right over Brown's head, who resumed reading:

I wish to inform you that last Tues. I pushed a man under a train. The express from Brighton, it was of course late and no buffet service I believe. He was the first. This Friday, I'll kill a woman, without prejudice, extreme or otherwise. My mission, which I've decided to accept, is to teach the denizens of our little corner a lesson.

A lesson in manners.

Anyone, and I mean anyone, who behaves like an asshole in public shall be terminated. What people do in private is, naturally, none of my business. For research purposes, you might read Mr Candid *by Jules Hardy or* Blackstone *by . . . mmmm, the author's name escapes me; he kills people for similar reasons.*

A copy of this missive has been sent to the media. I don't want to draw them on you, but if we involve them at an early stage, maybe it's for the best.

Perhaps you'd be kind enough to inform your officers that they are not exempt from my intended cull.

Between us, Superintendent, we may create a tiny patch of civility in Southeast London. Is it too much to ask that in these uncertain days of fear, with cyberterrorists, ecoterrorists, and just plain terrorists, we may create a small area of 'forever England.' Who knows, it may catch on, and the country might learn a touch of refinement. Let's not get ahead of ourselves, eh? I'll do my part and, as a sign of my good faith, noblesse oblige if you will, I'm going to save you some valuable time.

I typed this on an old Remington I bought at a boot sale. Sharp, trained, and observant as you are, you'll have noticed the 'T' is faulty.

Brown hadn't.

This is not a clue, simply a faulty consonant. The paper I bought in Ryman's, like a million other customers (or so they'd like us to believe).

Fingerprints?

Alas, no. The old surgical gloves.

DNA?

*On the stamp . . . or the flap of the envelope . . . again
no. I used tap water.*

*I have provided one clue. Fair is fair, as we English tell the
Iraqis. No, silly, not my nationality. Do focus, that's not the clue.*

Porter suppressed a smile.

*The clue is the nom de plume. As the current idiom has
it . . . 'Wanna play?' I think a recent novel by P.J. Taylor
used that as a title.*

I digress.

Good will hunting.

Yours predatorily,
FORD.

Brown removed the pince-nez, literally flung the letter at
Porter, and said:

'Get on it.'

'Am . . . sir.'

The brusqueness was deliberate. Porter, not touching the
letter, asked:

'Is it right, no fingerprints?'

Brown was close to a coronary, roared:

'Course there're bloody prints; the postman, my secretary,
mine, and probably a hundred others, but usable ones?'

He banged his desk, asked:

'What type of moron do you take me for?'

There wasn't a civil answer to this.

Porter had gone to the pub and met Trevor, ending the day on a high note.

. . . but now I just listened—not liking it . . . but accepting the confessions as an unwelcome part of the deal I had made with myself.

—Charles Willeford, *Cockfighter*

4

HELLO AGAIN.

'Uptown Ranking,' remember that tune? Gets you juicing, gets that energy cranked. Yeah?

Had me a good one, sleep I mean. Took two Zanex with a double scotch, I was gone. Twelve hours straight.

You ever have to fly long distance, there's your solution. I once flew to Thailand, hadn't any pills, watched four movies cold. Yup, one after another. That'll put you in the zone, give you the old red eye. I think Jack Nicholson was in one or all of them. I flew Thai Airways, they keep you subdued with food. I went to Thailand to get laid.

Doesn't everyone?

Oh sorry, you probably love the culture.

Bollocks.

Try Paris, shit-head.

Whoops, I lost it there and I do apologize. But it does actually elucidate my crusade.

Which is:

To restore politeness. In Thailand, man, they have that shit down.

Even the flunkeys at the supermarket wear gloves and bow when you approach.

I shit thee not.

First few times, you're a Londoner, think he's taking the piss, might have to bang him up side the head. No, straight up, it's the real deal. What happens is, you get used to it. I mean, even the bar-girls, before they suck you off, ask permission. Like you're going to say no?

Then you get back to Blighty, the cricket's gone to shit, Beckham has yet another ridiculous hairstyle, and the first person you meet goes:

'Fuck you.'

Got me thinking.

Then my old man died and you know what? He was a gent. For real. Treated people with dignity and respect.

What'd it get him?

Rotten lungs and a fucking tin-plated pocket-watch, they really broke the bank on that one. My inheritance. Course, with his insides all messed up, he didn't get out. Once, two years ago, he'd managed to get to the local shop. Took him a time on the way back, with his *Racing Post* and Cadbury's Flake, he got mugged. Feisty old bugger, he fought back, that old English spirit of Dunkirk and 'Having a go.' Four teenagers, two of them girls, gave him a serious kicking.

Broke a bone in his face.

Bone.

When I'm on the streets, I watch the teens, watch for a group of four.

On my list, a cluster fuck.

Have a special adapted spray in a metal container. It's got acid in there, and a hint of ammonia plus a sprinkle of patchouli to add freshness to the carnage. Old hippies never die, they just molt.

I'll term it . . . delousing.

Newton Thornberg, *Cutter and Bone.*

Do yourself a favour, get down to Murder One on Charing Cross Road, buy it. You'll get a trace of who I am, where I'm coming from.

See all that Jonathan Franzen, Salman Rushdie stuff on your shelf, all those wanna-be Booker Prize contenders gathering dust, all that earnest shit:

BIN IT.

Get real, buddy.

You wanna know how the world works, get Andrew Vachss.

Not intellectual enough?

Get James Sallis, he'll fry your cells. Or for downright metaphysical, Paul Auster.

Crime writing, bro, it's the new rock 'n' roll.

Oh, I kept my word.

Offed a broad on Fri.

I was coming along the Kennington Park Road and a black cab pulled up, a woman got out, and the language of her. She was calling the cabbie every obscenity in the book. Then she flung the fare at him, brushed past me, nearly toppling me, so I thought, 'uh-oh.' Followed her, and she was on her cell, roaring at some underling. She turned into a large office building, and I was right behind. Up in the elevator, her giving large to some poor bastard all the time.

Off at the tenth floor and storms into an open-plan area, employees keeping their heads down, not wanting to meet her eyes, which was just fine with me. Slammed into an office and before she could bang the door, I was there. She glared at me, spat:

Who the hell are you? The tradesmen's entrance is at the rear.

I slapped her in the mouth, got a fistful of her hair, and dragged her to the window, opened it, and threw her out. I said:

'Learn some manners, you bitch.'

And then I just strolled on out of there. No one noticed me, no one called:

'Hey, what are you doing?' I mean this shit is so easy, talk about shooting fish in a barrel.

You ever hear a quote and you're not sure who said it, answer 'Mark Twain,' and 90 percent of the time, you'll be right. He seems to have said everything at least once. The rest was uttered by Oscar Wilde. Straight up, Twain did say:

'If the desire to kill and the opportunity to kill came always together, who would escape hanging?'

The first one, the guy, came about almost by accident. I was in Waterloo station, sitting in the café having a latte, and at the next table were a man and woman. He was berating her in a fashion that was astonishing. Like this:

'You stupid cow, how could you forget the messages? I told you a hundred times, get the bloody things.'

And it got worse. I won't trouble you with the vile stuff he said, it was in the vein of the above, only cruder. The woman finally got up, tears in her eyes, and fled. The other people in the place did what we all do, pretended not to notice, and so the likes of that prick flourish. I followed him out and he went to wait on the platform; the Brighton train was late and he was leaning over, muttering about British Rail. I came up behind him, pushed. Seemed kind of poetic.

There you have it, the first two, the grand beginning. Oops, there's the doorbell, probably my girl. More on her later.

It depends on a complete assurance that a punch on the nose will not be the reply.

—*The Raymond Chandler Papers:*
Selected Letters and Nonfiction, 1909–1959,
edited by Tom Hiney and Frank MacShane

5

FALLS WAS DRESSED for school, pressed her uniform, gave her sensible shoes a serious buff, examined herself in the mirror, grimaced as she discovered some new lines round her eyes. Tried opening them wide, worse, it seemed to deepen the ridges. Got in her makeup bag, covered them fast.

She was on her second coffee, no sugar.

Recently, her weight had begun to climb, and for one mad moment, she'd thought:

Ah, the hell with it, I'll score some snow, solve the whole deal.

The madness passed. Sure, she'd lose weight and:

Her job
Her home
Her mind.

Had been round that block more than once. A slice of Danish was perched beside the coffee-pot. Moving fast, she grabbed it, slung it in the bin, shouted:

'See if I care.'

A pile of notes, outlining the talk she should give at the school, was on the floor. She'd read them once, the very first paragraph proposed:

'The officer should immediately establish a rapport with the students.'

Yeah, right.

Like tell them where to score some Grade-A dope.

The wanker had obviously never heard of Brixton Comprehensive, the first on Falls's list. The 'students' were usually armed—knives, bottles, bats, sharpened combs—and the only rapport they sought was with the local crack dealer.

Falls knew the assignment was one step from the street. The urge to chuck, to walk, was overpowering. But, like Brant, the job was in her blood. Despite the previous years of disaster, she still got a buzz from being a cop. Nothing on earth equalled the rush of hitting the street. Brant knew, had said:

'You're an adrenaline junkie and no matter what rolls down the pike, this is the only work that gets your mojo cranking.'

A horn beeped, McDonald. She grabbed the notes, useless as they were, took a longing look at the Danish, headed out. A battered Volvo was at the kerb, McDonald behind the wheel. If she'd expected civility, she'd be waiting. She got in, said:

'Morning.'

Tried to put some warmth behind it. He gave her a look of withering contempt, muttered: 'Yeah, whatever.'

And hit the ignition, burned rubber, blasted into traffic.
Falls studied him as he drove. A shot cop is a gone cop, so police lore said. Had to agree when you saw the compressed lips
of McDonald. A native of Edinburgh, he'd been a hot-
looking guy, women referring to him as 'that hunk.'

Not no more.

He'd aged overnight, strands of grey in his once luxurious
hair. Deep lines along his cheeks, and a habit of grinding his
teeth. Add to this a simmering rage, and he was almost a
Brant clone.

Without the smarts.

Falls wondered why he didn't jack. The humiliation of
being partnered with her was like neon in his eyes, writ
mean. She asked as they pulled up outside the school:

'You want to run through this?'

'What?'

'For the kids, maybe lay down a plan of action.'

He turned off the engine, snapped at the keys, said:

'Here's a plan, fuck 'em.'

Falls, in her previous case, had had a one-night fling with a
lethal female bomber. She tried to blot out the memory. As
they approached the school, he suddenly stopped, asked:

'Is it true you slept with that cunt?'

If he'd pulled a knife, stuck it in her guts, he couldn't have
wounded her more. Inside, kids were roaring and running
along the halls. The scene looked like Bedlam unleashed.

Falls wished she was armed. And the first person she'd shoot was McDonald. A middle-aged black woman, weariness leaking from every pore, approached, asked:

'Is there a problem, Officers?'

She didn't address McDonald, but stared at Falls, black sisterhood in her eyes.

Falls said:

'We're here for the "Meet the Kids" scheme.'

The woman smiled, not from humour, but along the lines of 'You're not serious.'

She held out her hand, said:

'I'm Mrs Trent.'

McDonald ignored her, and Falls took her hand, felt the wetness that acute stress brings, said:

'Delighted to meet you.'

She offered tea and McDonald went:

'Can we get on with this?'

They could.

The class was composed of mainly black teenagers, a few Asians, and two whites. The atmosphere was hostility on speed. McDonald positioned himself at the back of the room. Falls had no choice but to go behind the desk, and try a cheery 'Hi, y'all.'

No response.

She got out the useless notes, began:

'The modern police force . . .'

And narrowly missed her eye being taken out by a flying missile. The class dissolved in guffaws as she lost her composure, began:

'Who threw that?'

One of the white kids, a wannabe Eminem who had to work harder to impress the black kids, sniggered, said;

'Bin Laden.'

Falls looked to McDonald, who was staring at his feet, as if he was someplace else.

He probably was.

Falls turned back to the class, said:

'We are not the enemy.'

The white guy shouted:

'No, you're just a cunt.'

McDonald was off his feet, sprinted to the desk, got the guy by the hair, and back-handed him twice, said:

'Shut your mouth.'

There was a stunned silence. The kid had tears in his eyes and McDonald stared at him, said:

'Hey, tough guy, you peed your pants.'

The black guys began to applaud, and McDonald bowed, said:

'That's police work.'

He then moved to the top of the class, Falls moving quickly aside, and he asked:

'Anyone want to know about the first fucker I shot?'

The rest of the session was a huge success and when they were done, the kids clamoured around McDonald, asking when he'd return.

As they left the school, the principal hurried over, said:

'What on earth did you say? They loved you.'

McDonald gave a smile, Brant-like in its cunning, said:

'I slapped one round the ear-hole.'

She gave the tolerant grin they learn in teacher training, based on grim fortitude, said:

'No, seriously though, if you ever give up police work, you have a real gift for communication. Might I get you some refreshments?'

No, they had to get on. The woman was still smiling as they drove away.

Falls asked:

'What the hell did you think you were doing?'

McDonald was attempting to overtake an articulated lorry but glanced at her, said:

'Doing? I thought I was saving your ass, that's what I thought I was doing.'

As he got by the lorry, he leant forward to give the finger to the driver, seemed delighted at the rage in the man's face. Falls said:

'You could cost us our jobs if that kid makes a complaint.'

McDonald gave a snort, which is a very difficult thing to achieve, you have to be very pissed off or nuts, then he said:

'Jobs! You call what we're doing work. It's the fucking

scrapings of the barrel, no one gives a toss what we do. A snotty-nosed wanker in a school in Brixton, you think anyone cares what he says? Get with the game, Falls. When the brass realize we're doing well, they'll take us off the detail, shaft some other bugger.'

She couldn't believe what she was hearing. Worse, she recognized the kernel of truth there, said:

'Yeah, and when did you get to know so much?'

What she was most bothered by was she'd admired his handling of the kid. She'd been panicked and now, now, for heaven's sake, she was beginning to feel hot for McDonald. Jesus, where did that come from? She hadn't felt attracted to anyone since Nelson, and he'd turned out to be a wash-out. McDonald was considering her question, answered:

'Where did I learn this? I'll tell you, getting shot helps.'

He paused as if he was reliving the moment when the gun had been in his face and the guy had pulled the trigger, added:

'I used to think, God help me, I used to think policing was about protecting them.'

He was gliding the car smoothly into a space, his eyes narrowed in concentration, and she prompted:

'Yes?'

'I now know it's about protecting us, usually from them.'

They were out of the car and she felt an actual weakness at the knees as she took full stock of him, ventured:

'You want to maybe get a drink or something later?'

A plane droned overhead and he looked up, then:

'You mean like a date?'

So okay, she wanted him and hadn't they just pulled it off as a team, so she smiled, softened her features, said:

'Yeah, why not. I could cook something. It's been awhile since I got domestic.'

He gave her his full blue eyes attention, said:

'Thing is, I don't fuck lesbians.'

"Play dead? Play dead? What the fuck's that all about? You want a dead broad, you just kill the bitch that way, you don't gotta pay her either."

—Nick Tosches, *In the Hand of Dante.*

6

PORTER HAD GONE into the pub and spotted Trevor straight away. He'd ordered a vodka and tonic, slimline, and got a full smile. Checked out the guy's butt and thought:

'Mmm.'

Trevor was changing a barrel and pushed that butt out to max effect, then looked up, asked:

'See anything you like?'

Took it from there. Porter hadn't been with anyone for ages and the sex was thus fast and fevered. Trevor, lying back in Porter's bed, asked:

'What, you just got out of prison?'

Porter gave a laugh, went:

'Hardly, I'm a cop.'

Trevor, familiar with the workings of the Met, said:

'They don't go to prison?'

'Not this one.'

So the relationship began. Trevor on leaving, with cab fare from Porter, said:

'I'm not a quick shag, I want something meaningful.'

So did Porter.

He didn't get back to Trevor for a time as he'd launched a full investigation into accidents during the previous weeks and, sure enough, two fit the so-called 'hits' that Ford claimed. The media had run with the story, proclaiming:

MANNERS PSYCHO ON LOOSE.

They were treating it more as filler, didn't really believe it was true. For this Porter was grateful; he'd a bad feeling that this was going to get very serious. Witnesses were none. Family and work colleagues of the two did concede that both victims were:

'. . . difficult, inclined to rudeness.'

The Super had Porter in again, asked:

'Is it true, did he kill two people?'

Porter moved cautiously, stammered:

'It's pos-sible, but we're still checking.'

Brown wasn't impressed, shouted:

'What's with the stuttering, is that a gay thing, a type of lisp coyness?'

Porter had to bite down, went:

'Sorry, sir, when I'm nervous, it happens.'

The Super looked as if he couldn't believe what he was hearing, shook his head, said:

'Get it sorted. I don't want this to escalate.'

Porter took a deep breath, ventured:

'Should we consider a task force?'

The Super rose out of his chair, a very bad sign, pointed his finger, and said:

'Task force? Are you bonkers? It's some piddling lunatic trying to get his moment of fame. Shut him down now.'

Porter wanted to ask: 'How?'

Settled for:

'Yes, sir.'

Outside he realized he was sweating, used a hankie to wipe his brow, and heard:

'Hot enough for you?'

Brant.

Porter tried to shrug it off, said:

'It's this Manners case. Probably nothing.'

Brant smiled, then:

'You ask me, it's going to run and run.'

Porter, horrified, said:

'You can't be serious.'

'Serious as AIDS.'

And was gone.

Brant was on a roll. He and Roberts had gone to meet with Caz, the snitch. Met him in a pub; as usual he was wearing a garish shirt. He wasn't happy that Brant had broken the rules and brought along Roberts. The whole fragile basis of snitching depended on one-to-one.

Brant was unfazed, said:

'So I broke the rules, get over it.'

Roberts was unimpressed with Caz and expected it to be a waste of time. He was wrong. When Brant asked about the car-ring, Caz not only knew about it but provided the address of the garage where the operation was and the names of the three central villains. Brant sat back and said:

'Nice one, Caz.'

Caz, fingering his gold medallion, asked:

'Do I get paid now?'

Brant nodded, said:

'The cheque's in the post.'

And they were out of there. Roberts had been scoring a hundred out of a hundred of his cases recently. No matter what he turned to, it seemed he had the Midas touch. Now, yet again, he was about to look gold. When the cops raided the garage for the hot cars, the first one they recovered was the Super's. He took Brant for a celebratory drink a few nights later. They went to a place on Charing Cross Road, newly opened. The owner was an ex-cop, and, whatever else, they'd drink free.

Roberts, to celebrate his success, had splurged on a new suit, bought in Marks and Spencer. He felt it was only right as their fortunes had recently taken a turn for the best. Winners together. He selected a brown pin-striped number as the salesgirl, who appeared to be from Bosnia, assured him it was the style of the season. He winced a little at the price, but what the hell, the sale of his house had given him a little extra and promotion was surely but a stripe away.

Brant appeared in a sweat-shirt that bore the logo:

EAT SHIT.

And stone-faded jeans that had a tiny hole in the knee. Roberts said:

'You're bloody kidding.'

'What?'

'I thought we were doing a class number?'

Brant fingered a tiny pin of a silver bird on his sweat-shirt, mocked:

'Ah, Guv, you think class is about clothes?'

He was forever hectoring Roberts that class was about exactly that, which was one of the reasons Roberts had laid out the small ransom for his suit. The ex-cop, waiting patiently behind the bar, smiled at the exchange. He knew all about Brant. Mainly that he was a contrary fucker. He was appalled that Roberts was wearing what appeared to be a shit-coloured suit. Brant looked to him, went:

'Jim-bo, a pint of your best ale for the star of the Met and a large Jameson.'

Roberts whined: 'I'm drinking beer?'

Brant, who was reaching for his Peter Jacksons, said:

'Sir, in that outfit, I'm afraid it has to be beer.'

Roberts was offended, asked:

'You don't like the suit?'

Brant gave it a full, intense scrutiny, and, his lip curled. He said:

'You really shouldn't buy stuff in the market.'

'Market? This is from Marks and Spencer. Do you know how much this cost?'

He could hardly get the words out from rage.

Brant reached over, felt the lapel, said:

'No wonder the shop is gone down the tubes. Was it on special offer?'

Roberts gulped down half the pint, said:

'Well, at least I'm not wearing torn jeans.'

Lame, he knew it was a poor retort. Brant fingered the hole in his jeans, seemed delighted with it, said:

'Bullet-hole, sir, line of duty and all that.'

There were times Roberts truly hated Brant, wanted to put a fist hard in his mouth and beat on him for an hour. This was one of those times. He said to the barman:

'Give me a large Bells and another of those Irish things for him.'

Brant was still staring at the suit, said:

'Don't worry, sir, the light in here, people won't see it too well.'

Roberts lashed down the scotch, said:

'Gee, that's a real help. What's with the bloody silver bird on your sweatshirt?'

Brant touched the pin with what appeared to be real affection, said:

'That's the laughing kookaburra.'

Roberts was seriously sorry he'd asked, went:

'Like that is supposed to make sense?'

'Aussie, sir, gets its name from its call, which sounds like mad laughter, a member of the kingfisher family, lives off snakes, mice, and lizards."

Roberts thought it was a good description of Brant. They took a seat and Brant immediately put the chat on two women nearby. As always, Roberts was amazed at how women responded to him, couldn't they see what a pig he was.

Nope.

Next minute they'd joined them and Roberts was sitting beside a fine woman with a see-through blouse. He could never figure out if you were supposed to look or keep your eyes averted. Brant solved the dilemma by saying:

'Lady, you are stacked. Is that the wonders of Wonderbra or just you?'

She was delighted and Roberts knew if he'd ever in his wildest dreams said anything similar, he'd have had a drink flung in his face. The second woman seemed as wild as Brant, which is saying something. She asked what they did.

Brant said they were accountants to huge laughter from the women, which encouraged Brant to add:

'A suit like my mate's, one of the perks of the job.'

A long, dizzy conversation focused on the merits of said suit and Roberts resolved to burn the bloody thing. When the women excused themselves to go to the ladies, Brant said:

'You're in for a ride there, sir.'

Roberts, determined to score some point in the evening, asked:

'And what if I don't want—as you so delicately term it—the "ride"?'

Brant was middrink, putting away double Jameson's like a good 'un, paused, seemed puzzled, then:

'You'll have to, just to prove a point.'

'Point? What bloody point?'

'To prove you're not gay.'

'What the hell are you saying?'

Brant seemed genuinely confused, said:

'I told them you were gay, and they said you'd have to be to get away with such an outrageous suit.'

Roberts was reeling. There were so many reasons to wallop Brant he didn't know where to begin, so he weakly croaked:

'Why on earth would you tell them I'm gay?'

'Tactics, sir. See, women love a challenge, you owe me, pal.'

The women returned, more booze and then a late-night dancing club.

Dancing.

Yeah, Roberts attempting to revive the dying art of jiving, Brant at the edge of the dance floor, a sardonic smile in place and his hand up the woman's dress, almost as an afterthought. Then Soho for dawn kebabs, which is the very worst idea on a feast of booze but seemed mandatory. Later, Roberts would recall hot, sweaty sex and veritable gymnastics from himself. When he surfaced the next day, around two, the very first thing he saw was his crumpled suit looking like elephants had stampeded it, and in the lapel a shining beacon, the bloody kookaburra, and he was definitely laughing. Roberts had bought a tiny maisonette on the Kennington Park Road, with a minute garden at the rear. Dying from his hangover, he'd dragged himself there and set fire to the suit, it burned fiercely as if it didn't wish to go lightly into the good day. The pin, alas, refused to catch fire.

'*FULL AS A GOOG.*'

Extremely drunk. Comes from the Scottish word 'goggie,' a child's word for egg. It is a variation on an earlier Australian phase in the same sense, 'full as a tick.' Later combinations include 'full as a Bourke Street tram' and 'full as a bull's bum.'

7

FALLS WAS OFF the school detail, as McDonald had pre-dicted. Because they did well, they were quickly transferred. McDonald was shunted to traffic, and Falls was behind a desk doing paperwork. Stuck in a tiny cubbyhole in the basement, her job was to sift through old cases, see if there was anything needed updating.

A nothing task.

Even if she found a case that might benefit from review, there wasn't a hope in hell that it would get attention. The squad was up to its neck in current stuff, so an old file wasn't going to be considered. Everyone knew she'd been banished. Her only hope was to bide her time and see if a chance came down the pike. She gritted her teeth, half missed the schools.

WPC Andrews was relatively new, had been under Falls's wing for a time, and then done well. Brant had given her a turn, as he did all the new women, then dropped her. She was now on foot patrol in Clapham. She'd reported for work and heard about Falls in the dungeon, as the basement was known.

She got a tea and a slice of Danish from the canteen, headed down there. Met Brant, who asked:

'What, you're a waitress now?'

She wanted to roar:

'Why didn't you call me like you promised?'

But knowing he had lost whatever interest he'd had, said:

'It's for Falls.'

He smirked, said:

'She's a loser. You don't want to hang with her, get tainted with failure.'

She had to fight the urge to toss the tea in his smug face, tried to rally, said:

'She's my friend.'

He gave a short, nasty laugh, went:

'Falls doesn't have any friends. You want to get ahead, get shot of her.'

Then he moved on, whistling the theme from *The Sopranos* and doing a surprisingly fine rendition. In the basement she approached Falls, who was near hidden behind a mountain of files, said:

'Hiya.'

Put the tea and Danish on the desk like a peace offering. Falls stared at the pastry like it was a bomb, said:

'You think I can eat that?'

When Andrews didn't answer, Falls looked at her. Only a woman would see that beneath the make-up was a bruise under her left eye. She asked:

'What's the deal on the eye?'

Andrews involuntarily reached her hand to it, then said:

'McDonald took me for a drink.'

Falls waited and when Andrews said nothing more, she asked:

'What, he bought you a drink then slugged you, that it?'

Andrews wanted to cry and thought, *Wouldn't that be just bloody dandy. Two female cops in the basement, weeping. Like a very bad episode of* Cagney and Lacey. She said.

'He didn't mean it, but he's under a lot of pressure.'

Falls had heard this a thousand times. The ones who didn't mean it were the most lethal, usually the killers. She'd been to the Rape Crisis Centre where such stories were the currency. She sighed, asked:

'Are you going to see him again?'

Andrews was tempted to lie, but if she did and Falls found out . . . so she said:

'He wants to take me out on Friday, make it up to me.'

'Yeah, this time he'll do it right, put you in the hospital.'

Andrews protested, said:

'No, he's promised and it only happened because he was shot. Normally he's a fun guy.'

Falls let it go, asked:

'Was there anything else? The work I'm doing is vital to the safety of London.'

Andrews looked at Falls's face, the bitterness appalled her

and she thought that maybe she should have listened to Brant. She began to move away, said:

'Well, if you need anything?'

Falls said:

'Need? What could I possibly need? My cup overfloweth.'

It was late in the evening, Brant was standing outside the station, dragging deep on a cig. Falls approached, asked:

'Sarge, got a minute?'

He looked at his watch, she noticed it was a Rolex and probably not a fake, he said:

'59 seconds and counting.'

She had considered many different ways of couching her request but decided to go the direct route, said:

'I need a knuckle-duster.'

He was delighted, gave her his full attention, said:

'Gee, aren't they illegal?'

She knew she'd have to dance, so tried:

'I'll owe you, of course.'

He flicked the cig high in the air, watched the lit curve, then said:

'Course you'll owe me, you already do.'

And he strode off without another word. She didn't know if that meant okay or go fuck yourself or what. The constant dilemma with Brant, never knowing how he'd jump, the only certainty was he'd use the information to his own advantage.

Lunchtime the following day, she'd returned to her desk in the basement after a lame lunch in the canteen, a low-fat yoghurt and black tea. Sitting on her desk was a McDonald's burger box. She thought, *Andrews. Would it be a Big Mac or a cheeseburger, and more to the point, would she be able to resist it? She'd have to have a word with the woman, tell her to stop laying temptation in her path.* Sitting down, she flicked open the tab and there, sitting on a burger bun, a fresh lettuce leaf adorning it, was a well-used knuckle-duster. The irony of the brand-name on the box and the object inside made her smile for the first time in ages. She marvelled anew at the amount of insight Brant had; He knew stuff before you did yourself. She slipped the weapon into her bag.

Roberts was in the pub, nursing a pint of Bitter, still hurting from his night on the tiles with Brant. The door opened and Porter Nash approached, asked:

'May I join you, sir?'

Roberts liked Porter, felt he was a fine cop and admired the way he handled his sexual orientation. Porter had been feeling extremely well, his relationship with Trevor was, not to pun too obviously, cruising, and the regular sex was positively rejuvenating. The only bad moment had been when, early in the morning, Trevor had found him with the hypo, asked, without too much shock:

'You're a junkie?'

'Diabetic.'

Trevor thought about it, said:

'Bummer.'

Later, he'd asked:

'Is it true that you have to be really careful about your feet, that if you get a cut, you could easily need amputation?'

Porter had stressed that it was rare for such a scenario to happen, but Trevor had already lost interest.

Porter now asked Roberts if he wanted a drink. He declined and Porter sat, said:

'Can I run something by you?'

Roberts nodded so Porter began:

'You'll know about this "Manner's Killer" or alleged killer. I've been checking on recent accidents and two last week might be termed suspicious.'

Roberts hadn't touched his pint, seemed content to stare at it, said:

'Tell me about them.'

'One was a drowning in a bath, hard to say if it was an accident till we get the post-mortem to see if alcohol or drugs were present. The second was a hit and run. I interviewed work colleagues, friends, and guess what?'

Roberts had familiarized himself with the case, lest he be called in, said:

'They weren't exactly the most popular people on the planet.'

Porter was impressed, said:

'Right, they were noted for their rudeness, treated the world like dirt.'

Roberts digested the information, said:

'Sounds like you've got a player.'

Porter began to bite at his thumb, a habit he had managed to break, then said:

'My big fear is another letter detailing those deaths. I've put the nom de plume, "Ford" in the computer and got thousands of hits but nothing usable, tried various acromyns, but zip.'

Roberts stood up, said:

'Well, you know one thing.'

'Do I?'

'Sure, the guy likes to play. Did you ask Brant about the name? He's got a way of cutting through the crap.'

Then Roberts was gone, his pint barely untouched. Porter continued to worry his thumb. He hadn't heard from Trevor in two days and wondered if the needles had spooked him. He decided to call round after work to the bedsit where Trevor lived. Meanwhile, he hoped like hell that the Super hadn't gotten any mail.

8

McDONALD WAS IN the car pool, leaning against a van they used sometimes for surveillance. Falls approached and he eyed her with distaste. She moved right up to him, and he said:

'Hey, you're in my personal space.'

She smiled, said:

'Like a bit of rough, do you?'

His eyes lit and he sneered:

'What, tired of women already?'

She looked round then pivoted, used her body weight to swing her right hand, and hit him in the left eye with the knuckle-duster. He fell back against the van and she turned, walked away, saying:

'That rough enough for you?'

Said there's always gonna be somebody out there killing bitches. Bitches and mo' bitches is gonna be dying all over the damn place, till you-all up to your damn ass in dead bitches.
—G. M. Ford, *Fury*

9

COPS LIKE NOTHING better than a real shiner, a black eye in all its glory amuses them endlessly. So next day McDonald was taking a storm of stick. His story was he'd had a dispute with a motorist. No one believed it, and sure enough Brant came swaggering along, looked at him, said:

'Motorists carrying knuckle-dusters, eh.'

Which told McDonald where Falls had got the weapon, but of course he couldn't say anything. Just add Brant yet again to his ultimate hit list. Then the Super summoned him and on hearing the motorist yarn asked:

'And you arrested him?'

'Mmm . . . In the confusion, he slipped away.'

Brown glared, went:

'Forgetting something, are we, Constable?'

'I didn't get the registration, as I said . . .'

Brown shouted:

'Sir, I didn't hear you say "sir" when you addressed me. Now I have to wonder if you're really cut out for this line of work. You seem to be exceedingly accident prone, not a good trait for a policeman.'

McDonald wanted to protest, say how he'd yet again been the innocent victim, but before he could even start to whine, the Super said:

'Get out of my sight, have a look at the security ads, I hear they'll hire any one.'

The desk sergeant assigned him to the snarl of traffic on Balham High Road which, if not the highway to hell, was definitely the Road to Perdition. As McDonald slumped off, the sergeant roared:

'And if someone wallops you, call the cops.'

Brant was having a pint of Guinness, a ham sandwich curling alongside. The door opened and Falls came in, asked:

'Can I sit?'

'Sure, but can you fetch?'

She sat. Brant indicated the sandwich, asked:

'Hungry?'

'Actually I brought you something.'

Produced a McDonald's box, set it carefully before him. He smiled, took a huge swipe of his pint, it left him with a cream moustache, opened the box. A cheeseburger. He lifted the bun, nothing underneath, and he asked:

'Something missing?'

She gave him the look, asked:

'You wanted fries?'

He grabbed the burger, took an experimental bite, chewed noisily, said:

'Not bad.'

The barman came over, went:

'Hoy, you can't bring food in here.'

Brant, midbite, said:

'Piss off, oh, and bring a large vodka for this young fox.'

The barman was newish and not familiar with Brant, but something in the way he spoke told him to leave it be.

He did.

Brant levelled his gaze on Falls and she thought, despite how she didn't want to think, *He's attractive in a mad dog fashion. Like a line of cocaine that is going to fuck you good, but the rush.* He said:

'McDonald had himself a traffic accident.'

She tread carefully, answered:

'So I heard.'

Brant fingered his Zippo, got a cig out, flicked a light, drew deep, said:

'Watch your back.'

She didn't have a reply so said nothing. He shouted at the bar:

'Yo, boy, let's get some action here before Tuesday.'

Then back to her, went:

'You want to pay your chit?'

She was surprised it was so soon, usually Brant gave you, if not a time of grace, then a time to stew. She nodded and he gave the wolverine smile, said:

'That's a girl, best not to be in bondage. So you can be a cunt, am I right?'

The barman was placing the drinks before them as Brant uttered the obscenity and physically recoiled as if he'd been slapped but said nothing, moved away fast. Falls took a deep breath, went:

'What did you say?'

'Here's the deal. For the next week or so, outside the station, I want you to behave like a total animal, treat people like dirt, insult them at every opportunity, be as bad-mannered as you can imagine, act like you're PMT. Think you can do that?'

She reached for her drink, took it neat without a mixer, needed to taste the bitter wallop of raw alcohol.

She felt it.

Brant had sat back, downed his fresh pint in nearly one swallow, belched, said:

'Ah.'

Falls had a moment of clarity, then a gallop of rage, and nearly spat:

'It's the Manners case, right? You want me to smoke him out?'

Brant was delighted, said:

'See, I knew you'd get it.'

She wanted to reach in her bag, take out the knuckle-duster, and let *him* 'get it.'

Without asking, she reached over, took one of his cigs, and to her amazement, he lit it for her. She said:

'A decoy, that's the deal, isn't it?'

'Exactly.'

She needed to chill and without a word got up, went to the bar, ordered a round of drinks. The barman tried to smile at her, let her know he was with her, but she blanked him and he thought, *Fuck her.* When she got back, Brant grabbed his drink, said:

'Here's to better days.'

She didn't join the toast, simply downed the vodka and now she was chilled, said:

'You're in no doubt I'll do it, despite the fact I've been down this road before and nearly gotten killed.'

He shrugged, said:

'What? You've got a choice? You're on the road to nowhere, I'm giving you a chance to get back in the game. And the last time, who saved your pretty ass?'

Last time had been the Clapham Rapist. McDonald was supposed to be back-up but didn't follow through. Without Brant, she'd have been history. Brant said:

'Get started right away.'

'What?'

'When you're paying for the drinks, give the barman a bollicking, get you in the mood, plus he needs a kick in the ass.'

Then he was gone.

Falls played it round and round in her head, trying to see a way out. There wasn't any unless she wanted to vegetate in that basement. As she paid for the drinks, the bar guy said, after he thought he saw a smile at the corner of her mouth:

'That bloke is a pig.'

Falls fixed her eyes on him, said:

'And a wanker like you would know? You aren't fit to be in the same space as a real man.'

She thought outside:

Good start.

10

BRANT HAMMERED ON Porter's door and it finally opened to reveal a sleepy Porter, going:

'What's the matter?'

'Nothing, I was in the neighbourhood, thought you'd give me coffee. Hey, you've got post.'

Brant bent down, picked up an envelope, handed it over. Porter took it, said:

'Come in, I guess. I'll brew some coffee.'

'And juice, you got some OJ?'

Brant flopped on the couch, his feet up on the coffee table, and Porter said:

'Please make yourself at home.'

Brant was already lighting a cig and Porter had to refrain from comment. He got the coffee and juice, said:

'I'm going to have a shower, you okay for a minute.'

'No toast?'

While Porter was in the shower, Brant examined his book-case. No McBain, but lots of psychology, poetry, and history.

Brant muttered:

'Heavy shit.'

He was on his second coffee when Porter emerged, smelling of aftershave and dressed in a dark, expensive suit. Brant whistled, said:

'Nice duds, you got another one of those, you might lend it to Roberts.'

Porter picked up the envelope, noted the typed address, and opened it, read, went:

'Oh, god.'

Brant was up, asked:

'What?'

Porter handed him the sheet. He'd gone pale, a tremor in his hand.

Brant read:

To Porter Nash

You are no doubt aware of my mission to restore manners to our manor, excuse the pun. I did caution your chief that the police would not be exempt from my crusade. I've had a few drinks in your local watering hole and alas, have to report that the barman, Trevor, has been consistently rude, aggressive to all and sundry.

I know you have a certain attachment, but I must play by the rules and I'm afraid I can't make exceptions.

Trusting this will not adversely affect our relationship.

Yours regrettably,
FORD.

Porter croaked:

'He's going to kill Trevor.'

And stormed out the door. Brant caught him at his car, grabbed his arm, said:

'I'll drive.'

Trevor's place was just off Clapham Common and Brant got there in record time. They didn't speak. Porter gnawed at his thumb till he drew blood. When they got there, Porter was out of the car and inside the building, Brant behind him.

He began to pound on a door and Brant wanted to ask:

'He didn't give you a key?'

But maybe not the time to discuss the dynamics of their affair. No answer. Brant said:

'Stand back.'

And launched himself, taking the door down in one. They piled into the tiny space, a bed in the corner. A figure rose up, going:

'What the fuck?'

Porter went:

'Trevor, are you okay?'

Before Trevor could answer, another head surfaced from the blankets and asked:

'Are we in trouble?'

Without another word, Porter turned and walked out. Brant stared at the two, then said:

'Nice morning for it.'

That's the way I do business. I step on the gas and come straight at you. My late husband, Omer Plunkett? He used to say, 'Sherri never puts no Vaseline on it.'

—Doug J. Swanson, *96 Tears*

11

ANDREWS MARCHED RIGHT up to Falls, went:

'Did you have anything to do with what happened to McDonald?'

Falls gave her the look, waited, then:

'You get to ask this just one time.'

Andrews didn't like the expression on Falls's face, but she was committed now so went:

'Did you?'

'No.'

Andrews wasn't sure how to proceed. Falls waited then began to turn, paused, moved right into Andrews's face, asked:

'And if I'd said yes, what were you going to do? If I'd helped you out, you were going to do what exactly?'

Then she moved away, heading for the door, when Brant caught her up, said:

'Terrific, you're doing exactly like I wanted, but one thing, could you keep it for civilians, you don't need to intimidate the good guys.'

Falls laughed, said:

'You're the one who once said there are no good guys.'

He considered that, then:

'You don't want to put too much stock in what I say. Oh, and could you lighten up on Porter Nash. He's had a rough day, might be nice if you cut him some slack.'

Falls got outside, she was feeling fine and wasn't about to let anyone ruin it. The truth was, she was getting a kick out of Brant's assignment, sticking it to people. It was a rush, behaving like you thought they were total crap. She might continue to do so even if they caught the psycho. Coming to work, she'd stopped in her local mini-mart for the paper and a guy was holding everybody up with a Lotto entry.

She'd gone:

'Hey, moron, you want to show some thought for people who work for a bloody living?'

He was stunned. He'd moved right out of the way. Then, parking her car, a woman had tried to beat her to the place and she'd rolled down the window, shouted:

'You want to mess with a policewoman?'

She didn't.

Falls reckoned it called for a celebration. She'd go to some pub she hadn't tried before and put the staff through their paces. She felt a pounding in her blood at the thought of it and wondered if aggression wasn't as hot as a line of coke.

12

BRANT WAS ACTUALLY buying a drink for Roberts, put his hand in his pocket and laid out money. Roberts asked:

'What's the celebration?'

'We're going to be on the case, the Manners thing. Porter is going to ask the Super for us to be assigned.'

'Why? Why on earth would he share it? It's a trophy gig.'

Brant took a huge draw of his pint, gargled, then sat back, said:

'It just got personal.'

Roberts figured Brant would explain in his own good time so simply waited and heard:

'He got a letter threatening his current squeeze and I was there to hold his hand, so bingo, he wants us on board.'

Roberts digested this, then asked:

'How did the psycho get his address, and why change his MO to write to Porter instead of the Super?'

Brant took another swig, wiped his mouth, said:

'He didn't.'

'What?'

'He didn't.'

'Didn't what?'

'Write the letter.'

'How the hell do you know?'

Then he saw the smile and as realization dawned, he said:

'Oh no, tell me you didn't. Jeez, Brant, you wrote the letter.'

Brant had finished his pint, asked:

'We having another or what?'

Falls had given the barman some serious grief and only stayed for one drink. As she left, she shot the guy a look of pure malice. She almost collided with Ford as she stormed out. He wasn't a man you'd notice. Average height. Light brown hair cut short and tidy. He was wearing a sports jacket, and the shape hid his muscular build. Unlike most men of his generation, his hair wasn't receding, and his face held no particular outstanding feature unless you got close and saw the eyes. They burned with a light that seemed almost welcoming until you realized that the welcome was drawing you into a place you never wanted to be. His age was late forties. He smiled at the barman and ordered a shandy, pint of, said:

'Have one yourself.'

The guy was still shaken from Falls, said:

'Thanks a lot. You see that black woman who just left?'

'No.'

'You're as well off.'

'Yeah? Why's that?'

Ford's tone was friendly, concerned without being nosey. He had perfected a way of not being remembered. The guy poured himself a small scotch, said:

'Cheers. Man, I was real nice to her and she tore a strip offa me for no reason, then claimed I short-changed her. When I tried to make it up, you know, said to have the next drink on me, she lost it entirely. Called me a bastard. This job is hard enough, a person shouldn't have to take abuse for no reason. You should have heard her.'

Ford gave a small smile, a hint of sadness in there, said:

'Sorry I missed her.'

And he was.

I didn't say anything for a minute. But I thought,
"That's what you think honey. I'm doing you a favour by not
beating your head off."
—Jim Thompson, *The Killer Inside Me*

13

WHOO-EE, SORRY I took so long to get back to you. Killing people is so time-consuming. Man, I wouldn't like to have to do it for a living, wouldn't that be a pisser? I'm glad it's purely recreational. I mentioned my girl earlier, so let me introduce her. Odd, I write that and in my head, the opening line of 'Sympathy for the Devil' begins to uncurl. Jagger said when they do that track, strange shit happens, like Hell's Angels stomping a guy to death at Altamont.

He's sixty now!

Fuck, how'd that happen? And still touring.

Might take my own show on the road, soon as I get my commitments squared away. I've been thinking of America. Get me a pick-up, rifle on the rack, dog in the front seat, a coonhound of course, Hank Williams on the speakers.

Americans appreciate a decent killer.

A whole industry devoted to murder. Grab me some of that. Chat with Larry King. I was watching CNN and an FBI profiler (yeah, them again) said they estimate that at any given time, there are four or five serials out there trawling the highways. In England, we're still caught up in the Ten Rillington Place, Nielsen, Brighton Rock drabness. Those guys convey:

Depression
Greyness
Rain
Dampness.

I mean face it, they're so fucking boring, the very worst of the UK. We need to, in the words of the BBC:

. . . Sex it up.

You're on to me, right? Asking:

'What's with the girl? Why aren't we hearing about her?'

So I'm stalling, so shoot me. Thing is I'm a little bashful, cross my heart and hope to die. Cos, okay . . . okay, alright already, she's a working girl . . . yeah, what you call a hooker. Her name is Mandy, and no mention of the horrendous Barry Manilow tune. We've been an item for three years. And yes, she still plies her trade, sees clients a few times a week.

I met her in a pub, thought I'd clicked till she mentioned the freight. Paid her and like most men, one way or another, I've been paying ever since. She was having a hassle where she lived so I let her stay with me. Then later, got her a small place of her own, and she services the johns there. I don't ever go there, it's her work zone, right? But I can see her, the place is right across the road. You're thinking:

'What, all he could get was a hooker?'

I like her, simple as that. If she gets lippy and they all do, I flash the green, shuts her right down. Like marriage really. She wants a fridge, I get a blow job. Just barter, capitalism in action. Lately though, her manners are slipping.

AND YOU KNOW WHERE I AM ON THAT.

Started slow. We'd be in a pub and she'd give the staff an earful. I'd ask:

'What's with that?'

She seemed truly perplexed, her elfin face creased in confusion, went:

'What's with what?'

'Giving the staff grief.'

A huge smile and she has great teeth. I know as I paid for them. She answered:

'Because I can.'

I still have all my hair. See the young studs losing it. What they do is, they shave it all off, like they've a choice. I want to shout:

'Who you kidding, you're fucking bald, get over it.'

I take real good care of mine. Palmolive, they have a conditioner, red in colour that gives a fine sheen. Reason I mention it is, it looks like dessert mousse, same colour, texture, even got them little bubbles.

Mandy has a passion for mousse, eats it by the bucketful, doesn't seem to gain any weight. I guess full-time sex burns off them calories. So when she's running at the mouth, I prepare a bowl of her favourite, lash in the mousse, strawberry of course, then deep-six the conditioner, stir to a frenzy. She puts it away in jig-time.

Who knows, might be even keeping her teeth white, it's a guaranteed cleanser. What it does is lay her fucking flat, stops that nagging pronto. But lately, her moods are getting meaner, I said:

'Jeez, you're becoming evil.'

Got the look then:

'It's those morons, in shops, in pubs, doesn't anyone take pride in their work?'

Rich, eh? From a hooker.

We were in a bistro at Waterloo and she sent back the zucchini three bloody times, gave the poor slob of a waiter a plate of verbals. I said:

'You need to watch it, you know.'

Her mouth full of bread roll, she went:

'Duh?'

'There's a guy out there killing people for exactly the type of behaviour, you're exhibiting.'

She knocked back the chianti as if it was the house plonk, sneered:

'That loser, he comes at me, I'm ready.'

I was intrigued, asked:

'Yeah, how's that?'

Rooted in her Burberry bag, cost me a bundle in Self-ridges, produced a small canister, said:

'Pepper spray.'

I smiled, said:

'That'll do it.'

The waiter was approaching, hoping to hell she'd like this effort. I thought:

Worst case, she can zap the help.

14

LAST YEAR, SHE went to Dublin, stayed three months, made a packet along Leeson Street. Said: Catholics were always the best clients, paid double for the guilt factor, and that the club scene was seriously hot. Did I miss her? Some. She returned with, I kid you not, an Irish accent and a dose of the clap. Don't know which was worse. To mark her return, we'd done the West End, some boring musical—one of Lloyd Webber's inflictions—and then an overpriced supper at the Café Royal. I was locked into my American phase. You can imagine the horror, Mandy murdering the brogue and me doing a cracker from the woods of Tennessee. Add a batch of Tequila Slammers and you had medieval carnage.

15

I'VE ADDED TWO since my last entry. Drowned a guy in his bath, had heard him in a shop giving large to a child who was crying, and followed him home. Checked him out for a few days then simply called at his house. He'd appeared in his bathrobe, going:

'What the hell do you want, I'm trying to have a bath here.'

I gave him a bath.

The next was a woman who worked the till in the garage on the Clapham Road, as ugly a person as you'd ever meet. Lashing out at customers like some dervish. Watched her for a while and she took her lunch the same time every day, so I borrowed a car from the lot, plowed her down. She turned at the last moment, saw my face . . . and from her expression, she'd no idea who I was and I'm sure my smile didn't help.

After that, to tell the truth, I got tired.

I'd been reckless, beginning to believe I could do whatever I liked, the sure way to get caught. I'd been incredibly lucky several times, and the cops only had to be lucky once.

So I backed off, concentrated on my work. I'm an account-ant, can you credit it? My old man used all his savings to send me to college, figured I'd be the success he wasn't. I'm very very good, found a knack for creative accountancy, crooked in other words, but smart with it. You want to hide money, I'm your man, you want to avoid the Inland Revenue (who doesn't?), then I'm your guy. Started out with a large firm but got so busy I had to set up private practice. You'd think it was boring, but hell, it's so exciting. Making money disappear is the ultimate trick. I'm an alchemist of the first order.

I was reading an article by Colin Wilson, he says that serial killers have an overwhelming sense of their own impor-tance . . . Whoops!

He adds that after studying them for forty years, they have one thing in common: a very high level of dominance. Oh dear, has old Colin nailed me there. I have to admit I was a little down after reading him. It's galling to be herded in with a group, and anyway, I'm pretty successful in both my areas of activity. But hey, hang on a mo . . . Shit, I'm doing it, trying to justify myself, a sure signal you're wrong.

This writing game has got me knackered. I thought it would be easy. One thing is certain, if Mandy keeps up her current level of irritation, she's history. If that's anger, fuck it.

'The only interesting people in the world are the losers,' she said. 'Or rather, those we call losers. Every type of deviation contains an element of rebellion. And I've never been able to understand a lack of rebelliousness.'
    —Karin Fossum, *He Who Fears the Wolf*

16

CALIBRE.

Brant sat back in his swivel chair and admired the title of his proposed book. Good macho ring to it. It had taken him a week to get that far, but he figured the best writers took a time. Mind you, he wondered how the hell McBain had produced over eighty books. He'd reread the 87th Precinct ones and figured if he just copied that style, he'd have the book done in a week. It looked so simple, just fill the pages with dialogue. He had Irish blood, talk was as natural as breathing, but fuck, he couldn't for the life of him get the shit down on paper.

Now that he was studying McBain, as opposed to just reading him, he noticed how very smart the man was. Brant had been raving for years about the books, but only now was he realizing how clever they were. The Q and A seemed to fill lots of pages in the book and didn't take up much room, that's what Brant liked best. He'd copied one of these, substituting Roberts and himself for Carella and Hawes, but it came off like a frigging kid's essay. Brant was rarely disappointed with himself, self-belief was his strongest asset. He knew his strengths and ignored his failings. Most things he shrugged away, muttered 'Kiss it off.' His history was littered with darkness, and the way he'd survived that was to keep it locked up tight. But if he was to write this goddam thing, he'd have to use the cases he knew. And they were beauties. He'd read up on 'Noir' and called it 'Nora.' He'd gone so far as to buy a book on 'Creative Writing' and after twenty pages of concentrated reading, slung it across the room, going:

'You're bloody joking.'

In the bookshop there were a heap of volumes with titles like *How to Write a Bestseller*, but he figured if they knew so much about it, how come they weren't writing the winners. The authors who wrote them, he'd never heard of, and if he knew one thing, he knew a con. He'd gotten the name of an agent and sent her a letter, saying who he was and his proposal to be an English Wambaugh. He didn't mention his real plan of wishing to be McBain. He knew most of these literary types were snobs; McBain wasn't intellectual enough for them. He said aloud:

'Gobshites.'

He'd had a reply and the agent said she was very excited about his project and could he send her a synopsis. What he wanted to reply was 'lashings of violence, sex, and negroes.'

His doorbell went and he was relieved, anything to get away from the writing. Brant lived in Lorn Road, a quiet street, just a mugging from the Oval. Most people on hearing the name wanted to add 'For' but didn't. He opened the door and there was Porter, looking the worst for wear.

Wearing one of those wax jackets that seemed a hundred years old, much favoured by the Royals. His suit looked like it had been slept in. Porter looked like he'd been slept in.

Brant asked:

'Got a warrant?'

No smile from Porter, so Brant said:

'Come in.'

Porter sat on the sofa, near sank in the depth, and gazed at the bookshelves, amazed at the amount of books. Brant and books didn't seem to go together. Brant said:

'McBain . . . I rebuilt my whole stock, took awhile.'

Porter was silent then asked:

'Could I get some tea, some herbal if you have it?'

Brant stood over him, asked:

'Do I look like a guy who keeps herbal tea?'

He went and got a pot of coffee going, added a little speed to the mix, just a tiny hit, get Porter cranking. Whenever Brant busted a dope dealer, he kept a little of their stock, and now had every pharmaceutical known to man. He found that a hint of amphetemine juiced up coffee like nothing else. Made some toast, piled on the marmalade, put the lot on a tray bearing the wedding of Charles and Lady Diana, then carried it to the living room. Porter had dozed off, so Brant kicked his ankle, said;

'Hoy, no sleeping on the job.'

Porter came to with a small scream, and Brant said:

'Incoming?'

Porter shook himself, and at Brant's insistence, drank the coffee. He said:

'I'm not really a caffeine fiend.'

Brant leaned over, said:

'Yo, buddy, you're fucked. Get some stimulant in you, that's why they say "Wake up and smell the coffee."'

Brant refilled the cup, asked:

'What the hell have you been doing, cottaging?'

Porter's eyes flashed. The notion that he'd trawl public toilets, though it was a fine British tradition, appalled him. He said:

'I've been sleeping in my car, outside Trevor's home, lest the guy comes after him.'

Brant waved his hand, went:

'You can pack that in, I've got it covered.'

Porter was surprised, asked:

'You have someone watching Trevor's. How come I didn't make them?'

Brant laughed, as if from resignation, said:

'Well fuck, if you could see them, they wouldn't be a whole lot of bloody use, would they?'

Porter considered—the caffeine and speed were racing along his veins, heading for a blitz on the brain—he was already sitting up, said:

'Thanks, I mean, god, for looking out for us . . . for Trevor . . .'

Brant knocked it off, said in a Brooklyn accent:

'Ain't no big thing.'

Porter spotted the computer and the screen with 'Calibre' in huge letters, asked:

'What's with that?'

Brant explained about the book and Porter asked for a notebook and pen and began to jot rapidly . . . filling pages like a crazed secretary, then stopped, said:

'Here's a synopsis.'

Brant was amazed, read it slowly, said:

'This is fucking brilliant. Was this one of your cases?'

Porter didn't quite know himself how he'd done it but felt it had to be done, the primal urge of the speedhead. He was standing now, the energy galvanizing him, said:

'No, it just came to me, to have a vigilante cop, you get him acting inside and outside the law.'

Brant read it again, asked:

'The name for the cop, Steiner, is that like Jewish?'

Porter didn't know, said:

'Why not, you have to have an angle, right, so the whole anti-Semitism will add tension to the narrative.'

Brant thought Porter was beginning to sound a little like the writing books he'd binned, but what the hell, he'd got the outline. Maybe get Porter over regularly, slip him some speed, and get a chapter a week.

Porter said:

'I'm nowhere on the Manners deal.'

Brant reluctantly put the manuscript aside, said:

'You've got to keep plugging away, check out every tip, talk to snitches, and you know what?'

Porter didn't, all he knew was he could run a mile, wanted to begin right now, could feel his feet moving. He asked:

'What?'

'Luck, pure dumb luck will probably break the case.'

Porter figured this was right but not something he could bring to the Super. He said:

'I'd better get going. Thanks for the coffee and it is probably the best I ever had.'

Brant smiled, said:

'Don't be a stranger, drop over more often, we can shoot the breeze.'

After Porter left, Brant typed up the synopsis, sent it off to his agent, could already see himself on chat shows, telling where he'd gotten the inspiration for his masterpiece. They'd ask if he was going to quit being a cop, and he'd get that humble look, say quietly:

'You don't ever quit being a cop.'

Maybe they could put it on the front of the book, put it on posters when they sold the movie rights. Brant was as happy as if he'd already sold the whole lot.

Henry said, 'I'm awfully short for a person. But I'm fun.'
—Robert B. Parker, *Small Vices*

17

FALLS WAS BEING reassigned. Brant had pulled her off the decoy gig, it wasn't working. She was before the duty sergeant, who said:

'I don't know how you got out of that basement. Once they go down there they're gone.'

She smiled, didn't answer. The sergeant figured she'd slept with somebody with juice and that might account for the smirk she was wearing. But he intended wiping that off, said:

'You're being partnered with Lane.'

PC Lane had been with the force two years, and his claim to fame or infamy was he'd been photographed with Tony Blair. That had looked like it might help his career, but recently it was a huge liability. Unless the Tories came back soon, he was doomed to obscurity, a pariah of New Labour proportions. His appearance didn't help. He was very tall and lanky, with an expression of friendliness, the very worst thing for a cop. The duty sergeant waited for a response from Falls, but she was too experienced to go down that road, she simply asked:

'What's the assignment?'

Disappointed, he said:

'There's a domestic in Meadow Road, the neighbours have been calling it in, get over there pronto.'

Falls wasn't wild about that 'pronto' but bit her lip. Lane was waiting outside, an umbrella up against a faint mist. Falls said:

'Lose that, you want to have some cred. At least look like you can tolerate a little rain.'

Lane folded the brolly and thought:

She's the ball-buster I heard about.

They didn't speak until they reached Meadow Road. A neighbour walking up and down, near spat:

'What the hell kept you, interrupted your coffee break, did we?'

Lane asked:

'Where is the disturbance, sir?'

The guy looked at Lane, thinking, *What a nerd,* said:

' "Disturbance," murder more like, it's on the first floor, apartment 1a.'

Lane looked at Falls, asked the question that nervous cops the world over ask:

'How do you want to play this?'

She was already in the zone, said:

'Carefully.'

They rang the bell, the silence from inside was ominous.

The door opened and a woman in her late twenties stood there, asked:

'Help you?'

Lane said:

'We've had a report of a disturbance, may we come in?'

She shrugged, said:

'The place is a bit of a mess.'

She turned and they followed her in. A small living room was strewn with broken plates, upturned furniture. The woman was dressed in a long, black chemise, Doc Martens, and had a bandana in her hair. Grunge by default. Falls looked down and saw a carving knife in the woman's left hand, held loosely. She nodded to Lane, said:

'Could I please have the knife?'

The woman lifted it, stared at it as if she'd never seen it, said:

'Sure.'

Handed it over, it was still wet with blood. Lane asked:

'Who else is here, ma'am?'

He was already moving towards the bedroom. The woman said:

'Just me now. I don't think Duncan is a tenant anymore.'

In the bedroom a man was lying on his side, wounds all over his body. Lane felt for a pulse, radioed for back-up, came out and raised his eyes to Falls, who asked the woman:

'What's your name?'

'Trish, though Duncan calls me "hon." '

Falls sat down near her, said:

'Trish, do you know what happened here?'

'Oh yeah, Duncan was taking my money. I hate when they do that, steal what's freely offered. So I stuck him.'

The coroner would reveal that she'd 'stuck' him fifty-six times. Falls asked:

'Would you like a cup of tea?'

She said she'd kill for one, which caused Lane to give Falls a worried look. Falls stood up, moved to Lane, said:

'Make the tea.'

He was shaking his head, said:

'Are you mad, she's a lunatic, she didn't stab that guy, she eviscerated him.'

Trish turned, said:

'Two sugars, please.'

Lane said:

'I'm going to cuff her.'

Falls moved in front of him, said:

'No you're not, you're making tea, got it?'

He'd heard the rumours about Falls and, with a sigh, began to search for the teapot.

Falls want back to Trish, and the woman asked her:

'What will happen to me?'

Bad things is what Falls wanted to answer, but said:

'Self-defence, you might get probation.'

Thinking pigs might fly. Trish yawned, said:

'I'll be glad to get a quiet night's sleep. Duncan snores, it really gets on my wick."

Lane brought the tea in a mug that had the logo

I'M A GAS.

After she took a sip, she asked Falls:

'You have a fellah?'

Lane was making faces of disgust, and she answered:

'No, not at the moment.'

Trish thought about that, then went:

'Is it a black thing?'

Falls wanted to say, isn't everything, but merely nodded. A few minutes later the heavy gang arrived and Trish was led away, calling:

'Won't you come and visit?'

Lane said:

'You've made a friend.'

'Fuck off.'

Back at the station, they had to fill out the myriad of forms that a murder entailed. Lane finished first and asked her:

'You want me to help you?'

She glared at him, went:

'Is there something in my body language that says, "Help me?"'

He shuffled nervously, tried:

'No, it's just I have a knack for flying through those things.'

She sat back, wondering why she was so furious, and figured it was because she felt sorry for the poor bitch who was going down for a long time, another casualty of the sexes conflict. She said:

'Fly through them, how about you take a flying fuck.'

He reeled back. He'd been warned she was lethal but felt their recent experience might have connected them. And worse, he fancied her so went for broke, asked:

'You want to get a drink or something later?'

She laughed out loud, said:

'Take a wild guess.'

He slouched away. Met Porter at the canteen, who asked:

'You okay?'

'Am, I think so. I've been partnered with WPC Falls and am trying to get a handle on her.'

Porter touched his arm, moved close, said:

'Don't bother.'

Porter bought him a cup of tea and asked:

'So what's this about you and Tony Blair?'

Lane sighed.

Brant had got a call from his informant, Caz, and met him in the Oval, across the road from the cricket ground. The sounds of the Test Series were a hum of comfort, if you liked the game, if not, it was solely annoyance. Brant had bought a copy of the *Big Issue* magazine from the regular vendor outside the tube station. Brant, still buzzing from his literary effort, gave the guy a five and said to keep the change. The guy asked:

'You going to the Test?'

Brant said:

"I'm Irish, I only follow hurling."

The vendor wanted to say:

'Fuck off to Ireland then.'

But he knew Brant was a copper and a rough one, plus he'd given him large, so he said:

'Great game.'

What Brant knew was it was a mix of hockey and murder.

Caz was already in the pub, wearing a garish shirt that had hoola hoops, naked brown women, and the logo

CHELSEA GOES RED.

A reference to the Russian billionaire who'd bought the club and was currently buying every player in the first division. Brant said:

'I didn't know you followed the footie.'

Caz was confused, went:

'I don't.'

Brant nodded at the shirt, and Caz said:

'I just liked the colour.'

Brant ordered a pint and said to the bar guy:

'Put it on the tab.'

The guy asked:

'What tab? We don't do tabs.'

'You do now.'

He sat, looked at Caz, who said:

'I can get you some of these shirts, at cost.'

Brant laughed, shook his head, and said:

'I wanna go spic, I'll let you know.'

Caz wasn't sure what this meant but knew he'd been insulted, with Brant what else did he expect.

Brant asked:

'So what have you got for me?'

Caz could hardly contain his excitement, had intended to draw it out and thus raise the value, but he blurted out:

'The Manners case?'

Brant was midswallow, had to put down the glass and act casual, went:

'Yeah, so?'

Caz felt the moment deserved his ethnic aspirations, said:

'Ees is big, no, mucho importante?'

Got a slap to his ear and the warning:

'Drop that wetback shit.'

Chastened, Caz said:

'I think I know who the guy is.'

Brant took out his cigs. The Oz were finished and he was back to Embassy. He missed those Australian packs. Lit up and Caz asked for one.

Was told:

'Bad for your health, but not as bad as fucking with me.'

Caz took a breath, said:

'There's a hooker. She says she knows the guy who is killing people.'

'Name?'

Caz felt his energy slipping, whined:

'Can we discuss reward?'

Another slap to the ear, so he said:

'Her name is Mandy, but she won't give it up for free. She wants paying.'

Brant smiled, went:

'She'll get what's coming to her.'

Caz slipped an address across the table, said:

'She won't talk to you alone; she insists I be there.'

Brant stood up, drained his pint, said:

'Don't welsh out on the tab.'

And was gone. Caz considered phoning Mandy, telling her it hadn't gone as hoped and warning her about Brant, then thought, *There's no warning in the world to prepare for that animal.* He began to root in his pockets to pay the freight.

In this city, things were happening all the time, all over the place, and you didn't have to be a detective to smell evil in the wind.

—Ed McBain, *The Big Bad City*

18

FUCK FUCK FUCK . . . sorry to start like that but I'm seriously pissed. And worse, I haven't killed anybody since last we talked. I screwed up, can you believe it? I can't frigging credit I've been so stupid. You've got a good idea of how smart I am by now . . . right?

Had it all together, chugging along nicely, killing at my leisure, a solid gig going, no waves. Putting it all down here in my diary. I mean you gotta keep a record, like I'm gonna do all this shit and be unknown. Be, as the profilers term it, 'an unsub.' Like Ford, when he realized the jig was up. I've followed him too closely and got screwed the same way. Yeah, a woman. Ford had it all together, Jim Thompson had it all down, then it all fell apart. I was so sure I had the measure of Mandy. Yeah, it's her, the treacherous bitch. I underestimated her. I keep this diary in a safe place, course I do, I mean I haven't lost the plot entirely. But I had it in my home, which I rarely do, and got drunk with her, passed out. Woke to find her about to leave and she was edgy, nervous, anxious to go. I asked:

'Anything wrong, hon?'

Man, she was jumpy, went:

'Ah, no, ah, I'm . . . late for the hairdressers . . .'

And she was gone. Lying through her fucking teeth. I know liars, having spent so much of my life practicing.

The diary, the journal, my goddam life is kept in a leather-bound volume that I bought on Charing Cross Road. Vellum parchment, the whole nine yards. Course, as a child of the movies, I'd laid a thin hair across the front, not that I for a moment thought anyone would have access, but I enjoyed the Bondish touch. The hair was gone, the book had been opened. She knew. I don't know if she had time to read it all but enough to send her flying. Considered going after her, nailing her on the street and doing her. But that infringed my code, the bloody code. It would spoil the whole deal I'd been arranging and, worse, I'd be exposed. So straightaway, I got out of there and down to Waterloo, hired a locker, put the diary in. Sweat fairly running off me, went to a kiosk, ordered a large crushed OJ. The assistant tried to flirt with me, going:

'Hot enough for you?'

I gave her the cold eye, said:

'I'm spoken for.'

And fucked off out of there, back to the flat to await the arrival of the cops because they'd be coming. Went round the whole area, seeing if there was anything to connect me besides the word of a hooker. She'd tell, oh yeah, she'd tell, and some dumb flat-foot would come barging in, sniffing round, and if he had the manners of a pig, I couldn't off him, least not in the flat. Women, the jails are full of suckers who trusted them, and me . . . Me! . . . I'd all the angles covered. And to think I thought I could best a hooker.

Deep breaths, concentrate, get Zen-like, get real chilled, think think think. . . .

Brant had considered telling Roberts about his lead, but hey, he had the car-ring going and good results from that. Porter needed the gig, so he called him and they met at Clapham Common. Mandy's place was near The Clapham Arms. Porter arrived wearing a black leather jacket, black pants. Brant was wearing his Driza-Bone. He had the Aussie hat but couldn't quite bring himself to wear it. He said:

'You look like a lethal priest.'

Porter didn't think this was flattery but let it slide, and Brant filled him in on Caz's story. Porter asked:

'What do you think?'

'Let's go see. He usually is on the money.'

The building was freshly painted and they rang the intercom, got buzzed in. Porter said:

'Not very security conscious is she? I mean she just let us in.'

Brant gave him the look, said:

'She's a hooker, what do you expect?'

Her door was open and she was waiting, dressed to impress. Mini-skirt and off-the-shoulder flimsy top, her hip cocked. Brant thought:

Man, this is one ugly cow.

In her late twenties, Mandy was showing a lot of mileage, the eyes verging on fifty years and up. Her skin was bad and her face was too long, she didn't have a feature you could appreciate. She said:

'You got ID?'

They showed the warrant cards, and she invited them in. The flat was neat if cheap, lots of very bad paintings on the walls and well-worn furniture. She asked:

'Get you guys a drink?'

She was relaxed, either she was used to cops, which came with the territory, or she was on something. They sat and Brant said:

'You have some information on the "Manners" guy.'

She smiled, sat, letting her skirt hike up. Porter she pegged as gay, but the other, the brutish one, he took an eyeful. She'd address him:

'So, you sure I can't get you something?'

She wet her lower lip, this usually got the Johns hot. Brant was staring, thinking she really was one ugly broad and did he detect an Irish accent? Asked:

'You Irish?'

This delighted her, and she knew she'd selected the right cop to focus on, answered:

'Would you like me to be, you like the colleens?'

Porter felt his patience going, snapped:

'You have some information or not?'

She glared at him then back to Brant, said:

'This punter, I've been doing him for three years, twice a week. He thinks we're dating. I read this journal he keeps, fancy leather book, it said in there that he killed people.'

Porter felt his spirits rise, wondered if they could be that lucky, prompted:

'And?'

She looked at him as if he was dense, said:

' "And!" I got the fuck out of there. If he's killing people, I'm not hanging around. Anyway, he woke up.'

Brant felt his excitement take a dive, asked:

'He knows you read the journal?'

She looked nervous, as if she'd messed up, then:

'I don't know for sure, but I got out of there, and he's been ringing me like all the time. So I told Caz. He said I might get a reward.'

Porter tried to curb his anxiety, said:

'Tell us about him, anything odd?'

Now she laughed, said:

'Other than killing people? He's a businessman, does some kind of figures or shit. He's got lots of money, I know that.'

Brant smiled at her, asked:

'He like anything kinky, he into that?'

Now she was offended:

'I don't do weirdos, no golden showers or any of that, not even whips. Course, a girl can always be open to suggestions from the right man.'

Porter said:

'Here's a suggestion. Give us his name and address, how does that work for you?'

She opened her mouth, looked at Brant, and made a silent miaow, was well pleased with this. Brant gave a non-committal nod.

She rose slowly, moved to the window, and Porter was hoping maybe she'd jump. She lifted the curtain, said:

'Right over there, see the large posh building, he lives on the ground floor. His name is Thomas Crew. He likes to watch me receive my customers.'

Brant moved over, gave her ass a quick pinch, keep her stupid, and asked:

'You think he's home now?'

She sighed, whether with delight from the pinch or exasperation was open to doubt. Did the American accent and badly:

'Like I'm supposed to know?'

Brant smiled, said:

'You should be an actress, got a real talent there.'

She moved a little closer to him, cops were good friends to have and this one had an animal allure, said:

'You think a working girl isn't acting like all the time.'

Porter near shouted:

'This Thomas, he ever mention the name "Ford." It mean anything to you?'

She really was cross at him, interrupting her moment with the animal, and said:

'Duh, did I say his name was "Crew," did I?'

Porter moved towards the door and Brant said:

'You go ahead. I'll join you in a moment.'

Porter felt his sugar-level dropping way down, and with diabetes that was serious. Anger and stress didn't help the condition much either. Ten minutes before Brant appeared, and he had a shit-eating grin, Porter asked:

'What?'

Brant fixed his pants, said:

'For an ugly cunt, she sure has a lovely mouth, who'd have guessed.'

Took Porter a moment before the penny dropped and he asked, near shocked:

'Oh, come on, you didn't . . . Jesus, I mean . . . you wouldn't?'

Brant gave him an innocent look, said:

'Never look a gift hooker in the mouth.'

WPC Andrews couldn't believe it, she was hooked up with McDonald. The desk sergeant glared at her, asked:

'You got something on your mind, Constable?'

She shook her head, what could she say. McDonald didn't look any happier, but these days he always looked like that. The sergeant said:

'There's been a complaint about noise in a flat on Cold-harbour Lane, the local residents are making waves. So get over there, sort it out.'

Andrews wanted to ask if it was a good idea to send two white cops to Brixton but followed McDonald as he headed out. As she struggled to keep up with the rapid pace he was setting, she asked:

'Am, how've you been?'

He never looked at her, answered:

'Fucking hunky-dory.'

And that nailed that.

Brixton, as usual, was teeming, and they got lots of snide remarks as they moved through the crowds. Coldharbour Lane was unusually quiet, and McDonald asked:

'What's the name?'

'Name?'

'Yeah, of the person we're supposed to be cautioning.'

'Oh.'

She had to consult her notebook, not easy at the pace he was maintaining, and he said:

'Before the winter, yeah?'

'Jamil, he's in the ground-floor flat, Number 19.'

McDonald grinned, said:

'Jamil, bet he votes Tory.'

They banged at the door and no reply, so McDonald gave a look around, then put his boot to it and it gave way. Andrews said nothing, simply followed him inside. Music was blaring from the first flat on the ground floor and Mc-Donald said:

'Jamil, I presume.'

The door opened and a white woman came crashing out, screaming obscenities, stopped on seeing them, and went:

'Oh . . .'

Andrews asked:

'Is Mr Jamil at home?'

The woman stared at her as if she couldn't quite believe what she was hearing, then: 'Mister . . . That is fucking priceless, but if you mean the no-good, lying, cheating bastard who think he's Bob fucking Marley, then yeah, Mister Jamil is home . . . and receiving guests.'

She gave a hysterical laugh. Andrews didn't know who Bob Marley was, her tastes tended to Beyonce and J.Lo. The woman headed for the street, said:

'Bust his ass good.'

McDonald said:

'Sounds like grounds to enter.'

And went into the flat. Andrews felt this was definitely one of those times to call for back-up but followed anyway. The smell of weed hung in the air like cordite. African spears, shields, knives lined the walls. It took them a moment to see through the haze. Sitting in a low chair, back to the wall, was a bald man, black as coal, dressed in shorts only. His body was slick with oils. The music was deafening. He peered at them through slit eyes, said: 'You muthahfuckahs want?'

McDonald moved to the music console, turned it off. The silence was total, then the man asked:

'The fuck you doing, whitey?'

McDonald moved to the table, picked up a bag of weed, said:

'You're busted, bro.'

The man smiled, displaying gold teeth and a scarlet tongue. He looked at Andrews, said:

'Yo a foxy bitch, yeah?'

Andrews tried to take charge, said:

'If you'd care to accompany us to the station.'

Even McDonald turned to look at her. In the moment McDonald looked away, Jamil put his hands under the chair, produced a sawn-off, said:

'Surprise.'

McDonald couldn't believe this was happening again. He remembered the last time he'd stared into the barrel of a gun. The seconds before the guy pulled the trigger, sweat pouring off his face and the fucking awful pain. The months of rehabilitation and the fear, the sickening, creeping fear. His body started to shake, and Jamil said:

'Y'all want to turn on my music again.'

McDonald turned to the console then ran for all he was worth, expecting shots in his back, and he was in the street, drenched in sweat but unhurt.

Jamil seemed stunned that the cop had legged it, not half as stunned as Andrews, whose jaw had literally fallen. Jamil smiled, those gold teeth gleaming, the barrels swinging to her midriff, said:

'How dat song go? . . . "I Got You Babe." '

Well, whenever it gets too bad, I just step out and kill a few people. I frig them to death with a barbed-wire cob I have. After that I feel fine.

—Jim Thompson, *The Killer Inside Me*

19

ROBERTS WAS THE first to arrive at Coldharbour Lane, followed by the Heavy Mob, the tooled-up gang, ready to shoot on sight, the street sealed off and all the preparations for a siege being set. McDonald, still sweating heavily, said to Roberts:

'He's got a sawn-off, Andrews is there with him.'

Roberts stared at him, smelling the stink of desperation, asked:

'How'd you get to be out here?'

McDonald had been readying this since he'd called for back-up, said:

'I ah . . . managed to distract him, then went for back-up.'

Roberts's eyes, boring through him, asked:

'Let me see if I get this right. He has a gun, you distract him, then you take off. How'd that help Andrews?'

McDonald wiped the sweat from his eyes, said:

'It may not have been the best plan, but it was on the spur of the moment. I mean, better than him having two hostages, don't you think?'

Roberts looked round at the gathering force of coppers, said:

'I'd work on that story before you tell it again. The way it is now, sounds like you fucked off.'

McDonald had been praying that Roberts would buy the yarn. Now, in desperation, he said:

'I'm sure Andrews will back up my view.'

Roberts said:

'If she comes out, you think saving your ass is going to be her first concern?'

The door opened and McDonald heard the bolts on a 100 weapons rack, a sharp intake of breath seemed to course the street. Jamil was out first, his hands behind his back. Followed by Andrews.

McDonald had wanted to roar:

'Shoot the fucker.'

Roberts was running to the house, shouting:

'Hold your fire.'

Jamil was handcuffed, and Andrews gave Roberts a small smile.

In moments a wave of officers were all over Jamil, and Roberts led Andrews aside, asked:

'You okay?'

She seemed composed, said:

'Yeah, I think so. The gun was empty. He was so stoned, he'd forgotten to load it.'

Roberts looked at McDonald, who was hovering, asked:

'Did he actually squeeze the trigger?'

She turned, stared at McDonald for a moment, then turned back to Roberts, said:

'Yes, he did.'

Before Roberts could say anything, she said:

'I'm okay, really, you don't have to do anything.'

Roberts strode over to where the cops were holding Jamil and, without a word, kneed him in the balls. Then he returned to Andrews, and she asked:

'Would that hurt him a lot?'

Roberts nodded and she smiled. When they were hauling Jamil away, he managed to croak:

'Hoy, you, dee geezer dat ran. Yo leave dee sister to fend alone, yo dee criminal, man.'

Was heard loud and clear by all. McDonald tried to appear as if the guy was off his tree, shook his head in dismissal. Roberts said to Andrews:

'We've got to get you to the station. When a firearm is discharged, the brass want you to be debriefed. But I think a large scotch en route would go down nicely, what do you think?'

She seemed to be weighing this, then said:

'Could I have a large Vodka, with lemonade?'

Roberts held the door for her, closed it, then went to get in the driver's seat. McDonald was standing, at a loss, and Roberts beckoned him, said:

'The door of the house is still open. Could you close it?'

When McDonald seemed uncertain, Roberts added:

'You know, like closing the barn door after the fucking horse has gone.'

Then he slammed his door on McDonald and burned rubber out of there.

20

BRANT AND PORTER crossed the street, saw the curtain move in the lower window of Crew's house, and Brant said:

'Someone's home.'

Porter nodded, asked:

'What's your gut telling you, this the guy?'

'Yeah, this is him.'

They rang the bell and almost immediately it was opened. A man in his forties stood there, dressed in a waistcoat, pants suit, white shirt, sleeves rolled up, tie loosened. He was plain looking, not one feature to distinguish him, a face in the crowd. Full head of neat brown hair, regular features, average height. Slim build and a tension now in his body. To be expected, anyone opens the door to cops, you're tense. He said:

'Yes?'

Polite quiet voice but with confidence in it. They showed their warrant cards, gave their names, said:

'We're looking to eliminate people from our enquires, and your name came up.'

He studied them then asked:

'What enquiries are those?'

Porter looked back at the street, asked:

'Sir, might we do this inside?'

He nodded, stood aside, and they went in. The main characteristic of the place was how silent it was. He led them into a study lined with books, hundreds of them, shelves covering every wall. Brant said:

'You like to read.'

Crew put his hand through his hair, said:

'Who's got the time?'

His voice was subdued, cultured, but with a trace of authority. He indicated two armchairs, said:

'Please, sit down. Get you a drink? I'm about to have something myself.'

They said no, without the thanks, and while he fixed himself a scotch and soda, Brant walked along the shelves and made small sounds like 'Hah.' It was impossible to tell if he approved or not. Porter asked:

'You just finished work?'

Crew dragged his eyes from Brant, said:

'Yes, I am, as they say, something in the city.'

Porter found that annoyingly smug and let it show a little, asked:

'And that would be what exactly?'

Crew smiled, a smile of tolerance, asked:

'You don't already know?'

Porter was very testy now, said:

'If I knew, would I be persisting?'

Brant appeared oblivious to their wrangling, continued to book crawl, taking a volume down, putting it back.

Crew said:

'I'm an accountant, have a small office in the city. Here's my card, with the address.'

Porter took it, didn't look at it, asked:

'You know why we're here?'

Crew sat, took a slow sip of his scotch, seemed to enjoy it, then:

'I feel sure you'll get to it, lucky you guys don't work on a rate.'

Brant took a book down, said:

'Here's an interesting title, *"The Killer Inside Me,"* think I might borrow it?'

Crew shook his head, said:

'Breaks up my collection, so I don't lend books.'

Brant seemed amused, went:

'Ah, go on.'

Crew looked at Porter, said:

'Your sergeant doesn't seem to understand "no".'

Finally Porter got to ease a bit, said:

'Oh, he understands it, it's just he never accepts it.'

Brant left the book on the table, and Crew said:

'Could you put it back where it was?'

Brant fingered the spine, said:

'Seems well-worn, well-thumbed as you book lovers say.'

He put it back down. Crew waited and Porter said:

'You keep a diary, Mr. Crew?'

'Of course.'

They were surprised, had expected all sorts of denials, eva-sions, and for a moment, they were lost for a reply. Then Porter asked:

'Mind if I see it, sir?'

Crew stood up, moved to the phone, said:

'I wonder if I should perhaps call legal help?'

Brant was all charm, his voice friendly, went:

'That is of course your right but you show us the diary, we clear up a misunderstanding, and we're outa here. You go back to your scotch and soda and chill, no harm done.'

Crew frowned, asked:

'What is the misunderstanding?'

Porter took up the flow:

'A young lady, claims to be your . . . significant other, says she saw you mention an act of violence in your diary.'

Crew seemed astounded, said:

'Mandy, the . . . working girl I've had . . . am . . . recourse to . . . once or twice. That's why you're here. Good lord, clues must be scarce. The Met running out of actual crimes?'

Porter moved right up close to Crew, said:

'Three years she says, and you move her in across the street, hardly a casual deal, is it, Mr Crew?'

Crew laughed, a short bark, said:

'The word of a hooker, that's going to be solid.'

Brant asked:

'The diary?'

Crew went to his desk, a fine oak affair, and picked a leather volume up, tossed it to Porter, said,

'Enjoy.'

Porter flicked through it, looked up, said:

'This is your business diary; there's nothing personal here.'

Crew fixed another drink, less soda, said:

'For me, business is personal.'

Porter let that sit, then asked:

'How do you feel about manners?'

Crew looked puzzled, said:

'What on earth does that mean?'

Brant joined in, said:

'It's not a real difficult question, like, do you think they matter in the world, how we treat each other, is that a factor for you?'

Then Crew put his hand in the air, went:

'As Oprah says, "I'm having a light bulb moment." This is about that Manners guy, is that it? You think I might be the guy?'

Brant asked:

'Are you?'

Crew said:

'I'd like you to leave now. See, I'm asking politely, lots of manners, which is more than I can say for either of you.'

Porter moved towards the door, but Brant hadn't moved. He stared at Crew, asked:

'I can understand a guy using hookers, hell, it's part of the whole consumer society. But what I don't get is, you've got lots of cash. You look reasonably okay, yeah?'

Crew waited then asked:

'Is there a question there?'

Brant now began to move towards Porter, nodding, said:

'Well, it's not really a question, but given all I've said, how the hell did you go and pick such an ugly cunt?'

Then they were outside, and the door closed behind them. Brant lit a cig, said:

'You think he really watches Oprah?'

Porter was still looking at the door, said:

'Lots of guys watch her.'

'It's a gay thing, right?'

They'd got to Clapham Common. Brant put his hand in his pocket, took out a book, said:

'Now let's see what the deal with this is, why he was so keen for us not to see it.'

He had *The Killer Inside Me* in his hand. Porter yet again was astonished, went:

'You nicked it, jeez. You think he won't notice?'

Brant was flicking through the book, said:

'I want him to notice.'

Porter said:

'There's a nice café down here, they do really good coffee, you coming?'

He was.

Porter ordered a decaff latte and looked to Brant, who ordered a double espresso. Said he'd have the caffeine that Porter was skipping, oh, and bring him some really disgusting sticky, creamy bun.

Porter said:

'Are you serious about the pastry? The waitress doesn't know whether you're kidding or not.'

Brant, stuck in the book, said he was as serious as murder.

But little guys with wild hairs up their ass, there was no book on guys like that.

—Elmore Leonard, *The Big Bounce*

21

THE COPS WERE here. I fucked up and big time. Worse, I had a couple of scotches while they were interviewing me. And that blew my focus to shit. I got complacent, figured I could handle them easy. Two of them, Porter, the senior officer, and a sergeant named Brant. Porter I pegged as a fag. He had all that fussy manner, nice politeness, and the body language so I figured to concentrate on him. I figured the sergeant was just dumb. Figured wrong. If anything, he was the sharpest. Cultivates the animal persona. You reckon he's just pig-ignorant and brute force is the only game he's got. I should have known when he zoned in on the books. But no, I was busy playing mind-fuck with the fag. Next thing, Brant has "the book" in his hands, asks if he can borrow it? So I panicked and said he couldn't. Big mistake, now it was the centre of attention. When they asked for the diary, I got very stupid, gave Porter my business diary and acted all innocent. Pissing them off was not ever going to be smart and I just went right ahead and did it. Brant managed to distract me, so I never saw him pocket the book. They know of course I'm going to miss it, and thus they manage a double whammy. Think, damn it, think. There is no physical evidence, no way to connect me to the murders. Hell, they can't even prove the murders took place. A decent lawyer would blow them out of court. But I've got them interested in me now, and that's a real bad place. I wanted to play, but not up close and personal. The double act they had going tells me these guys are good. And my intuition says if they want my ass, they'll get it, one way or another.

So they read the book and, sure enough, it's going to sway them towards me being the guy they want. Can't be helped. I wish I could have gotten a few more killings under my belt before attracting notice. What's to be salvaged? Mmm, at least I know not to play at silly buggers. And the uncanny thing is, Ford, in the book, starts off so smart, so sure and undetected then, of course, the woman screws the whole deal, sound familiar? Jeez, I love the book, but I don't want to be the ending. What I want to do is get out there and off some fucker but tricky now my cover is blown to shit.

Brant put the book down, said:

'This novel, the main character is a sheriff, he kills people, likes to fuck with them, acts down home, friendly, and is laughing at everybody. Want to hazard a guess as to his name?'

Porter didn't take long, said:

'Ford.'

Brant smiled, said:

'No wonder he didn't want to part with it.'

Porter thought about it, said:

'Nothing we could bring into court.'

Brant had another look at the book, said:

'Least the fuck gets his in the end.'

Porter signalled for the bill, knew Brant wouldn't be paying, said:

'The murders can't be proved to be anything more than accidental, so what can we do?'

Brant was in no doubt, said:

'Lean on him.'

Porter wanted something solid. They were on to the guy, but so what? There was nothing they could charge him with. He asked:

'So we lean on him, what's that going to do, he's not going to confess.'

Brant was lighting a cig, blew the smoke out slowly, said:

'You lean in the right way, things happen, always do.'

Porter put a few notes on the table, said:

'I'm going to re-examine the killings, see if there's anything to join the dots."

Brant stood up, said:

'He knows we know, that is something.'

'But does it help us?'

Brant had no idea, said:

'I've no idea, but be sure of one thing.'

'What's that?'

'I'll get this guy, you can put that in the bank.'

Porter didn't like the sound of this, emphasized:

'You mean "we," right? We're going to get him?'

Brant hesitated, then:

'Sure.'

22

ANDREWS WAS BEING touted as a hero, the papers had got hold of the story and the headlines went:

PETITE WPC TACKLES ARMED DRUG DEALER.

The gist of the story dwelt heavily on how pretty she was and how, facing down a crazed gun-man, she'd not only taken the gun off him but arrested him and prevented a siege. A photo made her look shy and vulnerable. The Super was over the moon. He'd had a call from the home secretary and the George Medal was being hinted at. Brown took it as a personal vindication. He lined up the whole force and gave a speech extolling Andrews's outstanding valour. She was more than a little mortified at how it was getting so large, but secretly delighted, who wouldn't be. Dunphy, a hack from the tabloid, got a call from Jamil's brief, heard about the officer who legged it. His story got the front page next day:

HERO COP LEFT IN THE LURCH
BY YELLOW COMRADE.

It made no concessions and stated that McDonald turned and ran when Jamil produced the weapon.

Brown, trying to stem this, had McDonald in his office, asked:

'What the hell happened?'

McDonald, sweating freely, tried:

'I felt it was best to try and avoid a siege developing and grabbed an opportunity to fetch back-up.'

Brown stared at him, asked:

'That's it, that's your story?'

'I know it doesn't sound good, sir, but in the heat of the encounter . . .'

Brown cut him off, said:

'You cowardly bastard.'

McDonald had rehearsed this moment a hundred times, but in none of the scenarios was he out-and-out called a coward, the worst nightmare for a cop. Especially when another cop was involved, a woman. He tried to find some plausible line to get him off the hook but the word COWARD hung in the air like a death sentence. He remembered the movie *The Three Feathers* and against all the odds, the hero came back from such a charge and saved his mates. All this flew through his mind as he squirmed to find an answer. Realized the Super was speaking, heard:

'And not only are you suspended forthwith, but pending a hearing, I'm recommending you be thrown off the force as soon as possible. Now get the hell out of my sight and out of my station; you have a stink of weakness all over your miserable hide.'

McDonald heard himself say:

'Yes, sir, and thank you, sir.'

Jesus, he hadn't even the balls to tell him get stuffed. And as the man sunk his whole life, he was thanking him! He edged out of the office to find a bunch of officers outside, obviously having heard every word. He had to move through them, not one of them moving an inch. He got elbowed and pushed and was afraid to respond lest it get even uglier. The atmosphere was deadly, and he knew a lynching wasn't beyond the bounds of possibility. He got to his locker, his mind in tatters, opened the door, and recoiled. A dead rat hung there with the note 'Born to run.' He felt bile in his throat and thought he was going to throw up. Slammed the door and headed for the exit, a line of cops along the corridor, hissing quietly. He managed to get through the gauntlet, closing his ears to the taunts and jeers.

Outside, he took a deep breath. Roberts was coming up the steps, and before he could say anything, McDonald rushed down the steps, running as fast as he was able, doing the very thing that had landed him in all this hell. The lines of *The Gingerbread Man* echoed in his head, and he knew madness was detonating in his brain. He got to the pub, burst through the doors, said to a startled barman:

'Gimme a large Teachers and not one word of shit, you hear me?'

He heard him, it was hard not to.

The rest of the day was a haze to him, he moved from pub to pub and, odd times, he'd spy a cop on traffic duty or walking the beat, and he wanted to hide. The irony of his position wasn't lost on him, and it fuelled his rage. Instead of getting some understanding of how criminals felt all the time, he ranted in his mind at the injustice of it. If he could just perform one act that would catapult him into glory. He replayed the scene with Jamil a thousand times and always it came down to the barrels of the shotgun and the awful panic. He'd muttered to himself out loud a few times and noticed punters move away. He wanted to shout:

'Afraid? Of me? Hey, I'm a coward, nothing to fear here unless you want help and that's when I leg it.'

Wanted to weep and tried to think who he could call, no one, not a bloody soul.

Falls, she'd fallen spectacularly from grace, yeah, she'd fucked up big time and more than once, and here she was, she'd got her shit together. How'd she do that? Could he pull off the same miracle?

Towards evening, as it began to get dark, he headed towards Brixton, drawn back to the scene of his disgrace, turned into Coldharbour Lane. No one about. He looked over his shoulder and then went to the door, pushed hard and was in, stood in the hall for a moment and then entered Jamil's flat.

The yellow police tape on the door had already been stolen. He stood in the living room, closed his eyes, and could see Jamil level the gun at him, sweat poured from his brow. The whiskey he'd drank earlier had worn off, and he had a blinding headache. The flat was already tossed. The cops had only given it a surface search, but once they had Jamil, the impetus had shifted. McDonald began to search in earnest, doing the intensive sweep you only learned on the job. First he turned up a bag of coke, wedged in the freezer in a packet of fish fingers, plus a heavy gold bracelet. He had never done coke but knew the drill. Laid a line and used a five-pound note to snort, tickled his nose, and he thought he'd better do a few more to see what the fuss was about. Resumed his search and a few moments later was rocked as the dope hit. Felt the cold dribble along his throat and knew something heavy was happening, then he punched the air and said:

'Alright motherfuckers.'

And got the pure rush, had to stand still and let it wrap him in its embrace. The crystal-clear thinking began immediately. He felt strong, vibrant, the blood was singing in his veins and, speaking of songs, he wanted music. He found the remote control and faced the television. Wanted MTV and wanted it now. Chanced on the news, paused as the lead item was about a notorious pædophile, Graham Picking who, due to a technicality, was being released from what had appeared to be a slamdunk case. A whole list of children he'd molested and the evidence had been damning, no grey areas. Looked like he was going down forever, but a crucial item of proof had been lost and now the whole case was being thrown out. The screen showed Picking being led out by his grim-faced lawyer, who had the expression of someone who'd lost. Picking was mugging and grinning for the cameras. Something in McDonald clicked and an idea began to form. Almost at the same time, he noticed the right end of the heavy carpet wasn't quite solid. He'd never have seen it without the coke clarity, he was seeing a brave new world. Bent down and pulled at it, peeled it back and revealed two loose floorboards. Tore them up and BINGO. . . . A wad of money, large denomination notes, plus more coke, and items of jewellery. McDonald selected a heavy gold bracelet, got it on his wrist, liked the feel of it, and the prize, a Sig Sauer P226, 9mm. He said:

'Fucking A.'

Which was something he'd never thought in his life, nevermind uttered. Lifted the gun and loved the weight, he checked it and noted it held fifteen rounds. A stash of bullets also and he racked the slide, put a round in the chamber, aimed at the screen. Picking's face in his sights, whispered, 'Sayonara, sucker.'

Took him a real effort not to squeeze the trigger.

A mistake done twice is not a mistake, It's called failure.
—Robert Evans, *The Kid Stays in the Picture*

23

FALLS WANTED TO feel good about Andrews, tried to sell herself the sisterhood bullshit, when one woman succeeds, it's a victory for all women. Yeah, right. She was in her tattered bathrobe, sipping at tea, her day off, the papers in front of her. Andrews was on the front page of most papers, even The Big Issue had a feature on the deal. What galled Falls was how fucking humble Andrews looked. And truth to tell, she sure did have a pretty face. Next thing she'd be doing the sergeant's exam and talking about a shoo-in. Falls had failed it countless times. McDonald was sure fucked, though. Falls didn't see how he could possibly even stay on the force, she knew he'd been suspended and an enquiry was due. The poor bastard was gone, and she'd been so close to the door herself, she felt for him. She almost regretted the black eye she'd given him. When she'd mentioned him to Brant, who could save almost anyone, being a survivor himself, he'd sneered, said:

'He's gone.'

And Roberts, who'd been down the toilet a few times,

who'd usually go to bat for a cop, had compressed his mouth in a hard line, said:

'A yellow cop is a dead one.'

She thought of giving McDonald a call and say what?

'Tough shit, I hear security are always glad to employ a policeman.'

Maybe ask him if he'd like to go out, have a few drinks, but God, what a night that'd be. No, scratch that. She detested McDonald, had had so much aggro with him, she'd lost count. But she hated to see any cop go down. She sighed, took a sip of the cold tea, and tried to figure out how she was going to rise to a level of congratulations for Andrews. She'd just begun to like her too, they'd shared a few memorable moments, but that was over now. You couldn't hang with a hero, the light would blind you. Falls stood, picked up the papers, and dumped them in the trash.

Crew was tired, trying to figure out his next move and stay ahead of the cops was exhausting. It was like he had to think for three, himself and the two cops. They were coming and that was a given. Plus he had to show up at the goddam office. Being the boss helped, but he still had some major league pissed-off people on the phone, going:

'When am I getting my audit?'

Accountancy shit and when money was involved, as it was here and heavy, the pissed-off factor rose accordingly.

Wouldn't it be grand, as the Micks say, if he could tell the truth, go:

'Hey, I'm trying to kill people here, you wanna give me some fucking slack?'

He was sorely tempted. And he had serious plans to implement if he was to win this game with the cops and stay out of the nick. His secretary, Linda, had been very upset:

'Mr Crew, clients are demanding to know when they can get some time with you?'

Demanding!

That definitely was in the realm of bad manners. Wouldn't that be a hoot, kill his client base. Certainly be a first. God knew, the majority of them needed killing. Money only seemed to bring out the very worst in folk. He'd reassured Linda he was on top of his game. Which particular one he didn't specify. Mandy, the treacherous cow, wasn't taking his calls and wouldn't answer the door either. Man, it would be a downright pleasure to punch her ticket. He locked himself in his office, began the process of escape. Took some time and when he emerged, exhausted, Linda was moaning, he said:

'I believe it's time we gave you a raise.'

Shut her the fuck up, money rang the changes each and every time. Enough to make a chap cynical. He was always glad to get out of the city, the financial centre bored him. He liked money for what it could do but didn't see it as sexy or hot the way these new young guys spoke about it. Once he went with a few of the youngbloods to a wine bar and they drooled over the amounts they made, the number of dots on a pay-cheque. One of them, seeing his disinterest, asked:

'What gets you going, Crew?'

As per public schoolboys's rituals, they addressed you by your surname, which he considered the height of bad manners. He looked at the guy, a wanker in a very expensive suit, sweat under the arms of his Jermyn Street shirt, and replied:

'I like to make a killing.'

They conceded he was droll and never asked him again. He steered his BMW carefully under the limit, conscious now that any infringement of laws and they'd grab him. He eased the car safely into his drive and unbuckled the seat belt, looking forward to a scotch and soda and the quiet contemplation of his future. As soon as he opened the hall door, he knew something was wrong, the sense of stillness was gone, somebody had been here. Thinking:

The bastards, breaking in while I'm at work.

Walked to the lounge and there was Brant, stretched out on the sofa, a glass balanced on his chest, cigarette dangling from his mouth. He turned, asked:

'Hard day at the office, dear?'

He dropped his briefcase from shock. Did they have him already? Brant was smiling, said:

'Gave you a bit of a start there, eh?'

Crew found his voice, asked:

'What are you doing here?'

'Intimidating you.'

Crew couldn't get a handle on it, tried:

'You're breaking and entering, unless I see a warrant.'

Brant swung his legs off the sofa, said:

'Boofhead.'

Crew had no idea what this was, asked:

'What?'

'Aussie, mate, means a stupid person. Are you a stupid person?'

Crew moved over to the phone, said:

'I'm calling the police, there are rules against this sort of thing.'

Brant said:

'Touch the phone and I'll break your arm.'

Crew stopped, looked at him, went:

'Are you serious?'

'Try me, shit-head.'

Crew considered running for the door, going for help, but Brant moved and kicked the door shut, said:

'Pour us a couple of stiff ones, there's a good lad, and we'll have a wee chin-wag.'

It was the casual violence in Brant's tone that was chilling, almost friendly, as if breaking your arm was a gesture of no consequence at all. Crew went to the drinks, poured two large Teachers, asked:

'Ice?'

Thinking, *What am I doing?* and thought, *Stalling, playing for time.*

He put the drink in front of Brant and gulped down a swig of his own. Brant smiled at him with something like affection.

Crew tried again:

'This is ridiculous. You can't just barge in, threaten me, and think you'll get away with it.'

Brant stood up, stretched, then took a hefty swig, said:

'Ah, that hits the spot. You don't know me, I take it, not my rep as they say. Well, it's a bad one, I don't play by the rules. They investigated me twice on suspicion of killing a suspect, as if I would. What I want you to know is, I know you're the killer, but the problemo is, it's going to be a bitch to prove it so I'm going to take you out of the picture.'

Crew realized his glass was empty, gasped:

'What?'

'I'm going to kill you, and here's the part you'll appreciate, it's going to seem an accident. Hey, what do you think, make it seem like the manners guy got you, wouldn't that be a gas.'

Crew tried to get a handle on this, said:

'You're mad, this is insane.'

Brant smiled, nodded, answered:

'It is, isn't it, right off the chart. But tell you what, that ugly hooker, don't fret about her. I'll drop by, put a bag over her head, and give her the odd poke for you. How does that sound? You happy enough with that?'

Then he was heading for the door, added:

'I know it's a bastard when you don't know when I'm going to do the deed, but I've a fairly intense program. If I fit you in before the end of the month, would that work for you?'

Then he was gone.

Porter Nash shouted:

'You did what?'

He and Brant were in Porter's flat, Brant had arrived with six cans of special and a bottle of wine, saying:

'The wine's for you. You guys like that shit, am I right?'

Porter was about to sip the wine when Brant told him about Crew.

Brant opened his second can, said:

'What, you deaf? I told him I'd kill him.'

Porter put the glass down, jumped to his feet, went:

'You can't be serious?'

Brant wondered why it was so many people were saying the same thing. Did they doubt his sincerity? He belched, asked:

'Do you mean, did I seriously say that or do I seriously mean to kill him?'

Porter tried not to notice Brant's boots on his couch, it would be such a gay thing to comment. So said:

'Both, for heaven's sake. You can't threaten him like that.'

Brant was genuinely confused, asked:

'Why not?'

'Because you're a bloody policeman for crying out loud.'

This made no sense to Brant, who said:

'All the more reason.'

Porter wondered, not for the first time, if Brant was truly insane. He'd seen enough evidence of it, but this, this was pushing the envelope way past any perimeter. Then an even worse thought hit and he asked:

'You wouldn't, oh–my–god, you wouldn't take him out, I mean, come on?'

Brant was opening his third can, getting a nice buzz going, adding to it was Porter's tight-ass attitude. He hadn't had much crack for a while, but this was more like it. Fucking with people. He wondered why mind-fucking had such a bad rep? He decided to push a little more, said:

'If he got whacked, you think anyone would give a shit?'

Porter downed a glass of wine. It went against all his sensibilities to gulp wine, but this was rot-gut. And besides, dealing with Brant you needed some fortification, if only to try and navigate the landscape of the absurd. He shuddered as the wine hit his empty stomach, and Brant smiled. Porter said:

'Anything happens to Crew, I'm going to have to look closely at you, you're aware of that?'

Brant loved it. It was even better than he'd imagined, said:

'You're threatening your buddy, "your non-judgmental, even if you're a fag" buddy?'

Porter tried another tack, said:

'He'll report you, what then?'

'Who'd believe him? I mean you're having some difficulty and I've told you straight.'

Porter threw his hands up in the air, it was like trying to talk to an alien, they were so obviously speaking different languages. Brant stood, said:

'I gotta run, it's been fun, but I'm knackered. You need to relax, you worry too much.'

At the door, Porter asked:

'Tell me you won't do it?'

Brant seemed to consider, then:

'Well, it won't be tonight. I'm too whacked. You need to be fresh for that line of work.'

After Brant had gone, Porter poured the rest of the wine down the sink, brushed his teeth to rid himself of the taste. He thought about Trevor, and he missed his company. His sugar levels had been through the roof recently and the last visit to the doctor, he'd been told to cut down on stress. And wouldn't you know it, the other day he'd been flicking the pages of the newspaper and, sure enough, came across a case of a man with diabetes who'd had to have his leg amputated. Stress that.

He decided he needed to eat and set himself the task of peeling potatoes, cutting and washing vegetables, then lightly grilling a piece of fish he'd bought in Selfridges. Not too many cops shopped there, which was one of the reasons he went there regularly. In the kitchen he was struck by how everything he was doing was singular, all for one person, and that struck him as very, very sad. He continued with the task though he'd lost all energy for it. Went to his drinks cabinet and selected a nice dry white, cost a packet at the wine outlet. Used the corkscrew slowly and lovingly to extract the cork and let out a sigh as he heard the satisfying 'plop.' Went to a top shelf, got a heavy crystal glass, went to the sitting room, and laid the table with a linen cloth, then got the silver holder, lit the one red candle, stood back to admire his work. The fish was done and he carried it out, set the one place with care, put the cutlery just so, poured the wine, asked:

'Is it as sir anticipated?'

He stood back, gently took hold of one end of the linen top, and pulled with all his might, the whole lot crashing across the room, the crystal glass shattering in bits.

Jamil was released on bail. The prosecutor lodged objections, but the judge, mindful of McDonald's actions and the huge press interest, allowed him to go. Outside the court, Jamil gave a speech to the TV, focusing on the injustices meted out to black people. McDonald watched at home, the Sig in his hand, three lines of coke in his system, and a fixed grin on his face. Flicked his wrist and the gold bracelet moved satisfyingly. He said:

'You're fucked, you bastard, and you don't even know it.'

He had his plan prepared, it had taken him a coke-fuelled night to put it all together. He'd kill the child molester and put the gun back under Jamil's floorboards, then he'd arrest Jamil, proving it was him who'd offed the child molester. This

would show that McDonald was involved in, not only catch-
ing a killer, Jamil, but indirectly, the child molester. So okay,
he knew there were a fair few holes in the scheme but overall,
it was solid, the coke told him it was marvellous, and besides,
he didn't have a whole lot of other avenues to explore.

His phone rang. He jumped and then took a deep breath,
picked it up, heard:

'McDonald, it's Falls. I a . . . wanted to know if you were
doing all right.'

He was stunned she'd call, the last time he saw her, she'd
walloped him and his impulse was to say go fuck yourself, but
hey, he needed all the help he could get so he said:

'I'm hanging in there.'

Then figured sympathy would be good as he hadn't had a
shred of it to date, added:

'It's rough. I feel as if I'm falling apart.'

She rose to the bait and he smiled as she gushed:

'I know how you feel, I've been there and it's the pits. Is
there anything I can do?'

McDonald focused, figured there might even be the pity
fuck in this, and he'd always wanted to have the black bitch, all
sorts of pay-offs were forming in his fevered mind so he said:

'It would be good to talk to someone.'

And then remembered that women loved this crap so he
added the buzz word:

'If only there was someone to share with?'

He was grinning now, this was how Brant operated and no

doubt, Brant was a winner. He could already picture it, the black cow under him, as he plummeted into her, giving it large, and nearly laughed out loud. She took the bait:

'Oh I know, that's the worst bit, not having anyone to talk to, the isolation is desperate.'

He had to take a moment to stop himself from guffawing, then:

'Would . . . would you talk to . . . me?'

And the crazy bitch jumped in:

'I'd be honoured. Would you like to have a drink this evening?'

He let a break enter his voice and was amazed, he never knew he had this shit in him, said:

'I'm . . . so grateful, thank you.'

Now he could hear her choking up, jeez, they'd have a bawl fest right here on the phone, sobbing like they were on Oprah. She said:

'The Oval. It's quiet on a Tuesday, say around eight, how would that be?'

'Thank you, I can't tell you what it means, I'll never be able to articulate my gratitude.'

'You're welcome and call me Elizabeth, okay?'

He wanted to say:

'Call me stud.'

It was a typical car service crew, evenly split between retired and retarded, with a few degenerate gamblers thrown in. Surprisingly, no drunks, but then maybe they'd hired me for my potential.

  —Tim McLoughlin, *Heart of the Old Country*

24

THIS COULD BE our last song together, oh yeah, I'm like history, I've enjoyed this diary but this is not only the final entry, it's THE END OF THE AFFAIR. If you've gathered how much I liked *The Killer Inside Me* and, if you've been paying attention, Ford was fucked, and his enemies closing in. But did he have an ace up his sleeve.

READ THE GODDAM-BOOK.

I'm looking over my shoulder as I write as time is like, really on the out. The cop, Brant? The one I figured was a lot smarter than he played it, well he paid me a little visit, yeah, on his own docket so to speak, and guess what? He's going to kill me! How fucking ironic is that? And yes, I believe him. You kind of had to be there. He's a psycho, an out-and-out lunatic, and what's worse, I think he's going to enjoy the act. He intends playing first, get me spooked, get me frantic, and he's succeded. As the Americans say, WHO AM I GOING TO CALL?

I can't believe it's all gone so pear-shaped, I was on a roll, just taking it nice and easy and then the woman blew it to hell. Like the aforementioned book. So what am I going to do? I'm getting rid of this bloody diary is what, but I couldn't resist a farewell entry. And like all the do-gooders ask, did I make a difference? Is this little corner of London more civilized, more considerate? I'm afraid not. Too little time, too many assholes.

That's all.

Last page of The Killer Inside Me *says: 'Yeah, I reckon that's all unless our kind gets another chance in the Next Place. Our kind. Us people.'*

—Jim Thompson, *The Killer Inside Me*

25

WHEN CREW EMERGED from his office at the end of an exhausting day, Brant was leaning against a car, toothpick in his mouth. Crew didn't know whether to ignore him but found himself drawn to approach. Brant didn't move, simply adjusted the toothpick in his mouth. Crew asked:

'Is this it, you're going to harass me?'

'Yup.'

Crew thought he detected a softening of Brant's attitude, asked:

'The other evening, what you said, you were messing with my head, yes?'

'Nope.'

'You can't seriously think you'll get away with that . . . that threat?'

'Sure do.'

Then Brant's phone rang and, almost lazily, without taking his eyes from Crew, he reached in his pocket, took it out, answered.

Crew took the moment to move away fast, looked back to see Brant listening intently. When he rounded a corner, he ran like hell.

Brant heard:

'Sergeant Brant?'

'Yeah?'

'This is Linda Gillingham-Bowl, the agent, you sent me your opening chapter?'

'Yeah, sure.'

'I love it and would like to talk to you about the manuscript.'

Brant thought, *There is no manuscript, you got all there is,* said:

'Terrific.'

'Would Browns in Covent Garden be suitable, say this evening at 6.30?'

'Great.'

'I'll leave your name with the doorman.'

'No need.'

'Excuse me?'

'Lady, there isn't a club in London I can't get into.'

She gave a laugh of delicious fright, said:

'Oh you sound so like your writing, I'm very excited about this.'

Brant had to know, asked:

'Your name, you made it up, am I right?'

She laughed again, said:

'Oh you are a card.'

Card. He'd been called all sorts of names and few of them flattering but a 'card,' no this was a first, he said:

'See you anon.'

Click.

Crew had disappeared and Brant had to make a decision, fame or villainy? He considered and went with fame, got in his car, checked his watch, figured he'd have time to get home, spruce up, hit Covent Garden.

Back at his place, he selected a bespoke suit (muted navy), white shirt (Armani), police federation tie (stolen), and brown shoes by Loake (impressive). Splashed on some cologne, Tommy Hilfiger, that he'd liberated from a pimp, and poured a small brandy, toasted himself in a full-length mirror.

'You writers, you just kill me.'

Called a cab as he figured he'd be putting away a fair amount of booze and the driver said:

'Nice suit.'

Brant agreed and said:

'Out of your league, pal.'

The driver thought 'cop' and 'pig' and was silent for the rest of the trip.

At Browns, Brant smiled at the doorman, said:

'I'm expected.'

The guy recognized the heat though not usually so well dressed, stood aside, said:

'Have a pleasant evening, sir.'

Brant decided this writing lark was paying dividends already. The lobby was as he'd hoped, full of old furniture, and he moved to the lounge where old people sat in older chairs, the smell of money underwriting all. A woman came towards him, and his spirits sank, she was in her fifties and how the hell could that be. She'd had a young voice on the phone. What kind of shit was that to pull? Dressed in an expensive suit, permed hair, and fuck it, goddam pearls. She gave a glorious smile, asked:

'Sergeant Brant?'

Her hand outstretched, he reluctantly took it, said:

'Yeah.'

He sounded as pissed off as he was. In addition to selling the book, which he hadn't written, he was also expecting to get a leg over. She was delighted with his surliness, said:

'You're even better than I'd hoped.'

And, still holding his hand, she led him to some leather armchairs, sat him down, asked:

'What would you like to drink?'

A waiter had materialized quietly, stood patiently.

'Large scotch.'

The waiter seemed pleased at the rudeness, as if it was what he understood. The woman said:

'You know what, I think I'll have the same.'

She had finally released his hand but now looked for it again as she said:

'I'm Linda.'

His last hope faded, the chance that maybe she was an as-

sociate and the real deal would show later. Brant studied her
and was not encouraged. He'd poled some old broads but not
this one, no way. Her face was like parchment and she'd had
some plastic surgery, bad surgery, it gave her that ricktus
smile. He said:

'You sound younger on the phone.'

Needling her. Didn't work, she said:

'Why, thank you, young man. You're quite the charmer,
aren't you?'

Yeah.

The drinks came and he could only pray she wouldn't say;
'Bottoms up.'

She said:

'Bottoms up.'

He didn't answer, just sank the scotch. She settled herself,
letting her skirt hike up, his stomach heaved and she said:

'I don't usually meet new clients myself, but your writing
has such an immediacy, is so fresh that I had to meet you.'

She then rattled on about her A-list writers, which would
have been impressive if Brant had ever heard of any of them.
The waiter arrived with another drink, and she looked a tiny
bit better to Brant. She asked:

'I must know, who are your influences?'

'My what?'

Oh, she adored him. He was so barbarian, so real, she said:

'Who do you read? What writers have made the most im-
pact on you?'

'There's only one. Though when I went to Australia, I read Bill Bryson.'

She thrilled:

'Lovely man, Bill. Not as caustic as Paul.'

Brant ignored that, said:

'Ed McBain.'

She waited, expecting a full explanation, but none came so she decided to get down to business, began:

'Crime fiction is selling very well and the fact you're a policeman, we should be able to market you without any trouble. When might I see the full manuscript?'

Brant sank the remains of his drink, definitely felt much better, said:

'When do I see the money?'

She gave another full laugh, said:

'I must say your directness is so refreshing. After I see the full work I'll be able to pitch it to a top publisher, and I'm certain we'll get a healthy advance.'

Brant was hoping to steer her away from the manuscript and asked:

'No cash up front?'

She went into a long and detailed talk on how publishing worked and half-way through, Brant interrupted her, asked:

'Why would I need you?'

She launched into the merits of having representation, and Brant let her wind down.

Said:

'Sounds like money for old rope to me.'

Her laugh had lost a lot of its merriment, and she reached in her bag, produced a document, said:

'This is the type of contract I'll be proposing. This is of course only a rough estimation but perhaps you'd take a look, get an idea of what's involved. I expect film rights will sell or at the very least, TV interest.'

Brant perked a little at this, but again she waffled on and finally concluded with:

'So, Sergeant, when can I see the manuscript?'

Brant smiled, said:

'If you'd like a nightcap, we can swing by my place, take a look at my opus.'

She thought that was super.

When Falls entered the Oval, she'd prepared herself for the worst. Expected to see a shattered McDonald, possibly cringing in the darkest corner, a hunted and haunted man. To her amazement, he was sitting at the bar, full of merriment, chatting and laughing with the barmaid. He was dressed in what appeared to be a new black tailored leather jacket, faded jeans, white shirt, and, if she wasn't mistaken, was that a pimp bracelet on his wrist? What the hell was going on? He saw her, shouted:

'Here's my girl.'

The barmaid gave her a sour look and who could blame her. McDonald was positively shining, he asked:

'Liz, what'cha having, babe?'

Liz!

She wanted to drag him off the stool and lash the bejaysus out of him. She said:

'Mmm, a vodka and slimline tonic.'

Could have bit her tongue to say 'slimline' in front of the barmaid who gave a sneering nod which echoed *slimline*, the subtext being, *like, honey, you think that's going to make the slightest difference?*

McDonald, waving a fifty note, said:

'Give my girl a large vodka, Stoli if you've got it, hit me again and, of course, one for your good self, bring 'em on over to the table, there's a sweetheart.'

He positively leapt off the stool, waved Falls ahead of him, and followed. Falls had done enough nose candy to know the signs and especially the behaviour when you poured booze on the mix. She sat and he sat opposite, a grin plastered on his face. She noticed the line of perspiration on his brow.

He produced a pack of Dunhill Luxury filters. She didn't know he smoked and thought this brand had disappeared, said:

'I didn't know you smoked?'

He winked, said:

'There's a lot you don't know, babe.'

She leaned over and, to her horror, he seemed to think she was going to kiss him. How much of the white powder had he snorted? She said:

'Don't call me babe, don't call me Liz, okay?'

His smile faltered but the shit in his system took it in stride, and he laughed:

'Whatever you say, toots . . . whoops, sorry, it's just I'm so up.'

She stared at him, said:

'Yeah, I noticed.'

The barmaid brought the drinks, leaned over to let McDonald see cleavage, put the change on the table, smiled, and said:

'You need me, just whistle.'

That cracked him up, he looked like he was about to give her a slap on the rump, but she bounced away. Falls thought she'd throw up but instead picked up her glass and before she could get a sip, he raised his. Clinked her glass, said:

'To fallen angels and their triumphant return.'

She shuddered and knocked back a healthy amount. As he raised his glass, his jacket opened, and she saw the gun butt in the side of his belt. She asked quietly:

'Are you packing?'

Took him a moment to grasp the meaning then nodded solemnly, said:

'The fuckers are after me.'

No need to ask who they were, on coke, it was the world and any attendant demons.

His face was now deeply flushed and he rushed on:

'Bastards won't catch me napping. I'm frigging tooled.'

She stared at the bracelet, asked:

'What's with the jewellery, I didn't have you down as the type.'

He raised his arm, let the thing slide up and down his wrist, obviously an action he'd practiced, said:

'A soul brother gave it to me.'

She had no idea who this new McDonald was save he was out of his tree on dope. He suddenly jumped up, said:

'Whoa, gotta pee.'

And was gone like a bolt. Falls knew that deal, you were cruising on the coke and suddenly it roared, MORE. You rushed for the nearest toilet to refuel. He was awhile and she finished her drink, was considering a second, when McDonald returned, lit up like Piccadilly Circus. He signalled to the barmaid for more drinks, said:

'Your money's no good here, this is my show.'

He sat, shit-eating grin plastered on his face. Falls leaned over, wiped a smudge of powder from his nostril, said:

'You missed some.'

A moment as he watched her, then:

'A little something to help me out, you know how it goes. Shit, you wrote the book on the marching powder, am I right? You wanna do a little toot? Get you up to speed. I'm a bit ahead of you here and I need you up to gauge.'

He couldn't shut it, verbal diarrhoea poured out as the drug lashed through his system. He was off again:

'See, ELIZABETH, I've a master plan, and I want you in on it, get you some kudos too, gonna like share."

She sighed and the barmaid brought the drinks, a regular tonic, said:

'Oops, I forgot you were watching your weight, maybe you'll get away with one, live a little.'

Falls gave her the fish-eye and she took off. McDonald said:

'Gee, I don't think she likes you, how can that be?'

'Maybe because she's a stupid bitch.'

McDonald smiled, asked:

'A touch of the green-eyed monster, eh?'

Falls was all out of patience, said:

'Listen up, you're way off the chart here.'

'Alistair.'

'What?'

'My first name, it's Alistair.'

Falls sighed, she of all people should know you can't reason with a cokehead, stood up, said:

'You're seriously fucked. You get your act together, give me a call.'

He appeared stunned, whined:

'You're leaving, how can you be leaving, what about our sharing?'

Falls threw a poisonous glance at the barmaid, said:

'Tell her, she's interested.'

McDonald stood, went:

'But my plan, it's a winner.'

Falls shook her head and headed for the door. The barmaid shouted:

'You come back soon, hear?'

I have since learned that in the terminology of the recovery movement this is called 'being really fucked up.'
—John Straley, *The Curious Eat Themselves*

26

ROBERTS WAS ASSIGNED forgery detail. He was standing before Brown, the Super, and moaned:

'But, sir, isn't this territory for the fraud squad?'

Brown was having his morning tea, replete with a digestive biscuit. This was a ritual of horrendous proportion. He dipped the biscuit in the tea, then let it dribble into his mouth, a feat that required contortions that would have put off a lesser man. And the slurping sounds that attended this were enough to warrant justifiable homicide. Usually he performed this act in private but if he wanted to annoy an officer, he allowed them to share the spectacle. He really wanted to annoy Roberts. He felt the chief inspector was getting uppity; since he'd solved so many cases, he'd developed an air of superiority. Time to let him know who had the real juice. Brown said:

'There's been a rash of dodgy fifty notes circulating, and the brass want this sorted quickly. Since you're the whiz kid of the moment, I said you'd be glad to help. You are glad, aren't you?'

Roberts tried to turn his eyes away from the dripping biscuit, knew he was snookered, but went:

'I appreciate the vote of confidence, sir, but I hate to butt into another department's area.'

Brown rolled the soggy biscuit round his gums, his mouth open, said:

'You let me worry about that, that's what command is all about, just clear this up pronto.'

Roberts sighed, said:

'Yes, sir.'

He was almost out the door when Brown said:

'Tell my secretary to bring me another biscuit, this one was stale.'

Roberts rang the Fraud Squad, knew one of their guys named Foster, asked:

'Got a few minutes?'

Heard a low laugh and went:

'What?'

Foster was an okay guy, Roberts had had the odd pint with him and they'd walked the beat in the old days. Foster said:

'Wondered how long it would take you to call.'

Roberts was a bit put out, thought he'd have to go into a long spiel about meddling in their territory and he'd try not to step on anyone's toes, the whole grovelling gig. But here the guy was, expecting him. What was that about? Foster said:

'We'd a pool going here as to how long before you'd call, you just earned me a few quid.'

Roberts had found it cut the shit when you admitted you'd no idea what the hell was going on, so he said:

'What the hell is going on?'

Foster was still chuckling, asked:

'Dodgy fifties, am I right?'

'Yes, normally your manor.'

Foster said something to the squad in the background and there was a loud round of applause, then:

'Yeah, we handle bent currency every day, but when a certain Super gets almost arrested for passing a counterfeit note, you know he's going to get personal.'

Roberts nearly laughed himself, asked:

'Brown was burned?'

'Oh yeah, in a swanky club in Mayfair. Let's just say there were *hostesses* involved and no one spots funny money as fast as those girls.'

Roberts was delighted, anything that punctured that smugness of Brown's was good.

Foster was saying:

'So a chief inspector assigned to funny money, what a come-down.'

Roberts wasn't offended, asked:

'Tell me how to fix this?'

Foster stalled till Roberts asked:

'Okay, what do you want?'

The old barter deal, scratch my back or paddle your own canoe. Foster said:

'Be nice to have seats for the Test Series.'

Roberts groaned but in truth wasn't fazed, Brant usually had some spare, so said:

'That's asking a lot.'

Foster knew the deal was done said:

'And a case of some hooch, keep the nip out.'

'Sure you don't want a car to collect you?'

'Great idea.'

Foster then told him to grab a guy named Fitz, hung out in East Lane Market, but to tread carefully, the guy was volatile. Roberts asked:

'How careful are we talking here?'

'Tool up and bring back-up.'

'Enjoy the cricket.'

Roberts didn't think he needed back-up for some dodgy money character. Nor did he want help. What he wanted was to clear this nonsense and in jig-time. He headed for the market. Maybe buy some designer shirts too, spruce up his image; he certainly wouldn't be buying a suit. He figured he'd nail this fast, keep up his record of near full closure on all his duties. He was smiling as he thought of Brown, ogling a *hostess,* tipping her with a fifty, last of the big spenders, and then the consternation when the money was found to be bogus.

27

WHEN FALLS STORMED out of the Oval, leaving Mc-
Donald behind, she had a moment of total indecision. Her car
was parked at the church and she debated calling a cab then
said the hell with it, she'd drive. Got in the car, put the safety
belt on, checked her rear mirror, then eased out into traffic.
She was still seething with McDonald, the stupid bastard,
carrying a piece, coked out of his tree, and mouthing off.

Then she was rear-ended.

Went:

'The fuck is that . . . ?'

Stopped the car, tore out, ready to cripple whoever hit her.
A BMW was about a foot behind her, and a man got out,
wearing a very expensive leather jacket, not unlike McDonald's. She thought, what, there's a goddam sale of the bloody
things and the man went:

'OH-MI-GOD, are you okay? I am so desperately sorry,
all my fault . . . oh, you're gorgeous.'

She didn't know how to react, it had been so long since
she'd gotten a compliment that she was completely thrown.

The anger she'd readied leaked away, even as she realized that he was probably snowing her. Who cared when he was as gorgeous as he was. It was a long time since Falls had laid eyes on a truly handsome man, she'd forgotten the sheer thrill of it. He had eyes as blue as Paul Newman's and do they come any bluer? The guy's hair was dark brown, tossed in that way that costs a fortune. You pay the stylist a ransom to make you look like you ran your fingers through it, as if you couldn't be bothered. She wanted to reach out and touch it. He had a square jaw, wide mouth, and he was tall, with a slender build. His voice was deep, and clichéd though it was, he sounded like he was sincere. Now he said:

'Here's my card, my insurance will cover it, but might I be totally reckless . . .'

Here he paused, gave a self-conscious laugh, added:

'Good Lord, I've been reckless enough with my driving, but may I go for broke and invite you to a little dinner?'

The mood of madness seemed to envelope them, on one of the busiest routes in Southeast London. As drivers honked furiously he had her answer:

'Couldn't I have a big dinner?'

Signed, sealed, and delivered.

She parked her car, and he said:

'Give me your keys and your address. I'll have one of my staff bring it for repairs and have it outside your door in the morning. How would that be?'

Staff!

Better and better.

She wanted to roar:

'That would be fucking wonderful, you're wonderful, shit, life is a cabaret.'

And then she was in the front seat of his car, and they were en route to eat. She thought:

'Am I stark raving bonkers? He could be a serial killer and here I am, along for the slaughter, like a teenager.'

It gave her a delicious thrill. She hadn't been out on the edge for so long, it was a rush of almost cocaine level. He said:

'I'm Don Keaton, and forgive me for not shaking hands but I think I've had enough road accidents for one night.'

She clocked his hands, no wedding band, not that that meant a whole lot these days but it was a start. And his hands had a light tan, and looked strong, long fingers like an artist. She tried not to gush as she said:

'I'm Elizabeth Falls.'

Another first, she almost never gave her Christian name. He asked:

'Elizabeth, you like Italian?'

She'd have eaten vegetarian, said:

'Love it.'

He smiled over at her, said:

'I think you and I are going to get on good.'

She was already wondering if the sheets on her bed were clean. Wanted to say:

'Don, you just scored, babe.'

Calibre

After years of trauma, shitty luck, murderous experiences, here was the lottery all in one. He said:

'I've an admission to make, Elizabeth.'

She prayed to every saint she'd ever heard of:

Don't, for the love of all that's holy, don't let him be gay.

He said:

'I don't know any black people.'

And looked ashamed. She wanted to hug him, said:

'I'll be all the black you need.'

The restaurant was in Kennington, and the maitre'd greeted Don by name. When they were seated, he asked:

'The usual dry martini?'

Don looked at Falls who nodded and another waiter brought massive menus. Falls asked:

'Will you order for us?'

He did, a blaze of spaghetti alla chitarra, linguine, garganelli, taglierini, fusilli, and a whole pile of stuff she'd never heard of.

Don said:

'The house wine is especially good, or do you want to see the wine list?'

She didn't.

They ate like vultures, greasy, uncouth, and with passion. Half-way through, suffused with wine, he said:

'You eat like an Italian.'

She shook her head, said:

'No, like a person who'd been reared with hunger.'

It was the best night of her life. Don was a stockbroker and she asked:

'You mean like rich.'

He nodded and asked:

'And what about you, what do you do, Elizabeth?'

That moment.

Truth or dare?

Most times, she mentioned it, it distorted the balance, guys either got off on it, a weird gig about shagging a cop, a party dazzler, as:

'This is my black girlfriend, she's a cop.'

And the resultant queries, have you ever shot anyone or worse, the boy's own:

'Show me your truncheon.'

Or they got scared, took off. Mostly they took off. So she was silent for a second and he stared at her then she thought:

It's a magical night, go for broke.

Levelled her gaze, said:

'I'm a policewoman.'

He never faltered, straight out:

'That's wonderful, we need people like you.'

And so the evening of alchemy continued, she could do no wrong. Went back to his penthouse . . . yes, a penthouse on Mayfair, and fucked like demons. She had to put her hand on his chest, say:

'Whoa, let me catch a breath here.'

Her pleasure was his primary concern, and when did that happen? In the morning he drove her home, said:

'I might be falling in love with you, Elizabeth.'

She fell into her own bed, muttering:

'God, I owe you. Like BIG TIME.'

She slept the sleep of the truly contented, smiled in her sleep and emitted little groans of pleasure.

Roberts hadn't been down to East Lane Market for a long time and his first thought, was:

Where did all the English go?

The number of former Soviet nationals was staggering. It was packed and he recognized a pickpocket he'd arrested once. The guy named, originally enough, Dip, tried to pretend he didn't see Roberts. He began to move quickly through the crowd but Roberts caught him up, asked:

'Yo, what's your hurry, buddy?'

Dip acted surprised, went:

'Ah, Chief Inspector, good to see you.'

Roberts stared at him, the guy seemed down on his luck, shabby clothes and an air of desperation. The very last thing a guy in his line of work needed to look was desperate. Roberts said:

'Come on, I'll buy you a coffee.'

A stall was situated at the middle of the market, and Roberts got two roasting cups, said:

'It's hot, mind those fingers, eh.'

Dip took a sip, said:

'It's instant; I hate instant.'

Roberts laughed, he'd always had a soft spot for Dip, asked:

'How's business?'

Dip looked offended, tried for indignation, said:

'I don't do that no more.'

Roberts took a slug of the brew and burned his tongue, slung the thing away, said:

'You've gone straight, that it?'

Dip looked downcast, said:

'You can't try your luck with those non-English, you never know what diseases they might have and if you were crazy enough to try, you'd end up like that guy last week. He dipped a Croatian, got caught, and they sliced off his fingers.'

Roberts was smiling, the careless bigotry, racism from a pickpocket, the British Empire might be fucked but the spirit lived on in its thieves. Roberts asked:

'Do you know a guy called Fitz?'

Dip glanced around, as if they might be overheard, said:

'You don't want to fuck with him.'

Roberts realized this was the second time he'd been warned about the guy, said:

'He's a hard-ass, that it?'

Dip gave a grimace then:

'He's a bloody lunatic. You need that animal Brant with you if you're going to see him.'

Roberts was slightly offended, his pride was on the line, said:

'Where does this supercrook hang?'

Dip indicated the pub on the corner, gave a low whistle, said:

'He's always there but you've been fair with me, Mr Roberts, you cut me some slack before, so I'm telling you, call for back-up before you go after him.'

Roberts was moved, even if the remark came from a pick-pocket. Dip made to go and Roberts asked:

'How will I know him, in the pub I mean?'

Dip sighed, his expression saying:

I tried my best.

Said; 'You can't miss him, he's the biggest fucker in there and I mean size, oh yeah.'

Roberts had been a cop a long time and over the years, he'd taken some beatings, given some too. None were in the league of the one he received in East Lane.

Went like this.

He went into the pub, full of piss and vinegar. Brimming with confidence at the successes he'd recently achieved and figuring he was about to notch up yet one more.

He was wrong.

The bar was smoky, with Johnny Cash playing loud, 'Folsom Prison.' That should have alerted him. He misinterpreted it, thinking, 'fucking shit-kickers, English rednecks.' Men were in small packs all over the lounge and a hush descended as he entered. Not just because he was a stranger but these guys, dole scroungers, stall keepers, fugitives of all hues, smelt police. He spotted Fitz right away. He'd been told he was big, the man was huge, propping up the counter, midway through a dirty joke. He looked like a small mountain, a very mean one. Wild black hair, a grey beard, and and boiler suit. Not that he especially chose these outfits but little else fit his bulk. Like a Western, men began to move away from the encounter. Roberts, feeling powerful, asked:

'Fitz?'

The guy turned slowly, he had large brown eyes, with a mark below the left, as if someone had tried to gouge it out. His voice was surprisingly gentle, he said:

'Who's asking?'

Roberts smiled, it was classic, like the old days, everyone knew their role. He was going to enjoy hustling this moron into the nick by the collar, to fit the image. He said:

'Chief Inspector Roberts, I need a word.'

The barman poured a fresh pint of mild and placed it before Fitz, who went:

'That don't mean shit to me, pal.'

Loud nervous laughter from the hordes. This enraged Roberts, who'd been enjoying the whole scene, and worse,

Fitz lifted the pint and downed it in one fluid swallow, paused, then belched. Mild is wildly misnamed. It's usually the dregs of other beers, cheap and lethal. Roberts reckoned it was time to flex the blue muscle, said:

'Get your arse outside, I'm taking you in.'

And got the most ferocious wallop of his life, up under the chin, from left field. It lifted him clear off the floor, dropped him on his ass. Then Fitz wiped the stout from his upper lip, said to the barman:

'Have another pulled, I won't be long.'

Without effort, he leaned down and picked Roberts up by his shirt, buttons flying in all directions, threw him over his shoulder and walked out to the back of the yard. He threw Roberts aside like a doll, said:

'This is going to hurt like fuck, but you won't ever diss me again.'

Then he began to give Roberts the beating of his life. It didn't take long but it was relentless. Before he blacked out, Roberts heard Johnny go:

' "I shot a man in Reno, just to watch him die. . . ." '

28

BRANT ROLLED OVER in his bed, stared at the tousled head of Linda Gillingham-Bowl, man she looked old. But what a ride, she'd fucked him every which way but loose. And came back for more. He'd finally roared:

'Enough, I'll sign with you.'

Now all he had to do was get Porter to the flat, lace his coffee with speed, and get some more chapters out of him. Piece of cake. The phone shrilled and Brant shook his head, he was feeling the blaze of a medieval hangover but he'd enough medication to kick its ass. He lifted the receiver, croaked;

'Yeah?'

Heard Roberts was in the hospital and in bad shape. He jumped out of bed, got to the shower, and scalded the bejaysus out of his skin. Then to the medicine cabinet, got Solpadeine, a hint of speed, some Alka-Seltzer, and piled it in a glass with GALWAY BAY on the front. Added water and sunk it. His system fought like a demon to process the concoction. A moment between heaven and hell and then his stomach decided to go quietly and accept the verdict. He heard:

'Darling, where are you, sweet pea?'

He strode into the bedroom and she stared at his naked body, whistled low, went, 'You beast.'

He began to dress for combat. A battered leather jacket, faded jeans, and steel-toed boots. He said:

'There's coffee and shit in the kitchen, I gotta go.'

She reached out her withered arms and he suppressed a shudder, asked:

'Come pleasure me, you animal.'

He was already heading for the door, said:

'Keep it on max, babe.'

When Roberts opened his eyes, he felt an avalanche of hurt. Took a time to focus and then registered Brant and Porter Nash. Brant said:

'You stupid fuck.'

Roberts felt agony all over, tried:

'This is to console me?'

Porter looked angry, went:

'How could you go without back-up?'

Roberts didn't want to go there, said:

'It's a long story.'

Brant leaned over, said:

'Your nose is broken, your arm, countless ribs, and you have bruises on your face to make a cat laugh.'

Roberts was appalled, his lovely nose, his only decent feature, said:

'You should see the other guy.'

Brant nodded, said:

'Oh, we will.'

A nurse came, began to fluff the pillows, the mandatory nurse stuff, she asked:

'How are we feeling?'

Roberts said:

'I'm in pain, could I get something?'

'Not till the doctor does his rounds.'

'When is that?'

She looked at her watch, said:

'Oh, I'd say Tuesday.'

And was gone.

Roberts groaned and Brant put his hand in his jacket, said:

'Try this.'

A small brown bottle, with clear liquid. Porter was alarmed, tried to protest. Roberts asked:

'What's in it?'

Brant, impatient, answered:

'The fuck you care, you want to stop hurting or you want recipes?'

Roberts lifted the bottle and Porter reached for it, said:

'Sir, with all due respect, I'd wait till the doctor arrives.'

Roberts drank the potion, said:

'With all due respect, you're not hurting like a son of a bitch.'

Brant began to zip up his jacket, said:

'We've got to go pick up Fitz.'

Roberts was surprised:

'How did you know it's him?'

Porter shrugged, said:

'He called it in.'

'And he gave his name?'

'Yeah, even gave his address.'

They left, Brant goosed the nurse on his way out. By the time the doctor came round, Roberts was sitting up, singing 'My Way.'

In the car Porter asked:

'What was in the bottle?'

And got the wolverine smile and the answer:

'What else, "*Love Potion No. 9.*" '

Falls was having a rare moment of self-honesty. It was the day after her magical meeting with Don, when all her dreams came through. This morning a dozen red roses arrived from him and he'd phoned like six times. Everything she'd always wanted, right? Hell, he was the man the women's magazines eulogised and the hope of such a guy launched a new edition every week.

Every schmaltzy song was based on 'Mr Right' and the impossibility of finding such. He'd found her, crashed into her life.

So why wasn't she having all the symptoms of success, the runs, the pains in her stomach, the writing of his name on pages of pink paper, the linking of her name to his, how it would sound if she was his wife . . . All the insane shit that said: This is the real thing. Where was all that neurotic thinking? She'd made tea, toast with no jam, and only a thin spread of low-fat margarine and said aloud:

'He's got no edge.'

There, she said it, he was close to fucking boring, the constant adoration, who the hell was he kidding? Fuck, no one behaved like that unless they were on heavy medication. And his name? . . .

'Don?'

Was she supposed to think that was cute? She was raging, tempted to phone him, go:

'Why are you fucking with my head? Who put you up to this?'

And lit a cigarette, which reminded her, him saying:

'Oh, we'll have to wean you off those, my precious, can't have you damaging yourself.'

She hated him.

There, out in the open, enough said.

———

Graham Picking, the child molester, was very pleased with himself, getting off on a technicality, the pictures in the paper made him look hard done by. He laughed out loud. Combed his thinning hair, put some gel on there, make it appear thicker. He hadn't returned to his home, oh no. The neighbours would have placards and stones through the window. No, he was far too slick for that. Staying at his sister's flat in Islington, a school right down the road. He'd already made friends with the cutest little boy, a positively Botticelli angel named Ronan. He'd taken the sweets from Graham without any hesitation and would be waiting after school for the special surprise that Graham had pledged:

He remembered a phrase from an old TV show:

'How sweet it is.'

Tried to recall, was it *The Jackie Gleason Show?* He was dressed in a new suit, new shirt and tie, and shining black shoes. The picture of civility. He felt himself getting hard at the thought of the treasure to come. The first time you got them, oh the bliss of all that innocence. They knew you loved them, that it was pure love, not that soiled image the tabloids tried to present. He remembered when *The News of the World* ran the campaign of NAME AND SHAME . . . the pictures and addresses of his fellow travellers on the front page. Then OPERATION NEPTUNE, when the cops tracked down another batch of his fellows with the details of their credit cards from the Internet. He had to admit his chaps were foolish, trusting some chat room and some stranger to keep quiet.

If he wanted photos, and sure photos were good, he'd go down the Mile End Road, buy all you wanted, no details required but cash. He slurped a mouthful of coffee, sighed with near contentment. The sun was shining. He'd stroll down the street, buy the papers, and maybe some Danish in that bakery he'd seen.

Opened the front door of the house and a man was standing there. Graham panicked for a moment, thinking the media had found him. Then relaxed, this guy was wired, too wired even for a tabloid hack, seemed to be shaking, a Mormon who'd lost his marbles perhaps?

Graham said:

'Can I help you?'

Put some edge in there, have a little of the sucker's balls just for exercise. Then the guy's hand was moving, he had a heavy gold bracelet like a bloody pimp would wear, and then he saw the barrel of the gun, tried:

'Hey, wait a sec . . .'

The first shot took out his forehead and the second one, in his groin, blew a hole between his legs that gushed a fountain of blood. The splatter ruined the fine sheen of his black shoes.

29

JAMIL WAS SERIOUSLY pissed. Some fuck had been in his crib, stolen his stash, his piece and worse, his gold bracelet, it was like the one the guy wore in *The Sopranos*. He wanted to off some bastard, break into a man's home when he was in nick, how low was that? He had a spliff going, a major one, but even it didn't chill him enough to offset the loss of the gear.

A knock on his door and he grunted and figured he'd have the ass of whoever it was. Opened it to the yellow cop, the motherfucker who'd run. He was astonished, went:

'You?'

McDonald looked crazy, like he'd been on a blitz of heavy dope. He shot out his fist, taking Jamil under the chin, putting out his lights. Dragged him into the flat, got the weapon out and wrapped Jamil's fingers round it, then scattered coke all over the place. He wasn't wearing the bracelet, had with regret left it at home. Then he picked up the phone, called the cops.

Chaos.

The press, cops, the Super, Jamil's lawyer all arrived, and it took awhile to put it together. Sounded highly unlikely but the cops had passed fishier cases along. Don't mention the Birmingham Seven. The story that got issued as a press release went like this:

> PC McDonald, acting on a tip that Jamil had offed the child molester, arrived at Jamil's flat and the suspect pulled a gun, the same gun ballistics were able to prove that had killed Graham Picking.

It smelt to high heaven but the public, shedding no tears over Picking or Jamil, were delighted to have a hero cop and be rid of two scumbags. The cops didn't believe a word of it but were prepared to pull out all the stops to, not only reinstate a disgraced cop, but have two pieces of garbage removed. Smiles all around. If somewhat uneasy ones.

When Brant heard the story, he whistled in admiration. It was a scheme worthy of himself. He had no love for McDonald but didn't like to see any cop go down. He figured he'd buy the clever mad bastard a drink, it had been a plan so crazy that you had to sit up and go WOW.

Porter Nash was stunned, he couldn't believe the awesome audacity of the deal. Worse, somewhere in his mind was the mad notion that the cops were still the good guys, but this proved that they were seriously deranged. He was glad that McDonald was off the cowardice hook, and the image of the force, though highly suspect, was at least cosmetically okay.

But he felt a new low had been reached in the annals of the Met. Mainly, he was saddened. Sighing, he figured he'd do what he did best, continue to fight the bedraggled fight. He was going to wrap the Manners killer case today before Brant went and killed the guy.

He went out, hoping to hell he could wrap at least this one thing and do it clean . . . or cleanish.

Fitz, the beater of Roberts, had flown to Prague and was currently living it large, the only fly in his ointment that they didn't serve Mild. Roberts would spend fruitless weeks trawling The Costa Del Sol for him. Only when dodgy fifties began showing up in Eastern Europe did he begin to realize where Fitz was. Part of him kinda respected the guy.

Falls rang Don, went:

'Get the hell out of my life.'

And then she wept for three solid days.

Two days later Porter lashed at Brant:

'He's gone, Crew has disappeared, his bank accounts closed, the house up for sale, and because he's a bloody accountant, a paper trail is useless. Did you off him?'

Brant laughed, said:

'I should have but I got distracted. I didn't give him enough credit, he was slicker than I figured. What the hell, you win some, you lose some.'

Porter stalked off, too angry to answer. Days like this, he figured maybe he'd resign but Brant was calling him, going:

'Come round my place this evening, I bought you real coffee. I'll bring you up to speed, let you see my manuscript.'

Epilogue

IN THE DUSTY roads of Montana, a man named Wilson was hitching, hadn't seen a vehicle for hours. Then here came a pick-up and stopped. The door opened and a guy with a Limey accent said:

'Hop in.'

Wilson did, noticed a hounddog at the guy's feet and Hank Williams on the tapedeck. They drove off and Wilson, who didn't like Brits, didn't bother to say thanks for the ride. The guy had a paperback on the dash, but Wilson couldn't see the title.

The guy smiled, asked:

'Don't you have any manners?'

"Bruen is an **original**, grimly hilarious and **gloriously Irish.**"
—*The Washington Post*

KEN
BRUEN

Continue reading Ken Bruen with the award-winning series featuring Jack Taylor—a disgraced ex-cop battling addiction on the gritty Galway streets.

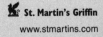